CUTS TO THE SOUL

JOYCE A SMITH

Reviews from readers of

CUTS LIKE A KNIFE

5.0 out of 5 stars
Cuts Like A Knife is a Double Edge Sword!
I was hesitant on beginning this book because my time is all over the place and my attention span is that of a two year old, but when I looked @ the cover and saw Lafayette Square, I was hooked. The memories from all the activity in the square from my childhood drew me to sit down and take moment. "Cut Like a Knife" was an great read, the characters had personalities like those of your friends and family. Your emotions are on a roller coaster. "Cut Like a Knife" is no exception; love between family, unlikely social economic statuses and twisted liaisons make your head spin as you reach for your glass of....................to mellow out the night! Cannot wait for the sequel because I got some questions I need answered and some people I need explained!

5.0 out of 5 stars
Great read.
This is an excellent book. The characters and the story line are intriguing and interesting. The authentic depiction of life in Baltimore is done in a thoughtful and creative way. I recommend this book for anyone interested in reading a book that will captivate and educate you at the same time.

5.0 out of 5 stars
Excellent Read
This is a great thriller. From the first page it had my attention, and it is now with great anticipation I look forward to the 2nd one (part two). This is the first I have heard from Joyce A Smith, but I feel certain it will not be the last from this creative and exciting new author. I highly recommend CUTS LIKE A KNIFE. It is her initial presentation.

4.0 out of 5 stars
Cuts Like a Knife
This book has it all! Love lost and love found, mystery and suspense. If you're looking for a sordid tale straight outta Baltimore, give this one a try. Hopefully, part 2 picks up the story!

5.0 out of 5 stars
Cuts Like A Knife -
I thoroughly enjoyed this book, and I'm sure you will too. It's a great read that holds your interest and will leave you wanting more.

5.0 out of 5 stars
I loved this book. I couldn't put it down. A must read. I'm waiting for part two. The storyline and characters are great.

Five stars
Excellent story! There were so many pieces, I couldn't wait to see how everything pieced together! Each chapter connected another piece. A must read. Loved it!!

5.0 out of 5 stars
Five Stars
Love the characters and story line

5.0 out of 5 stars
Five Stars
Well written; Thoroughly enjoyable read; True to life in Baltimore City; Looking forward to a sequel!!!!

5.0 out of 5 stars
A real page-turner!
An exciting and suspenseful book you won't be able to put down!

5.0 out of 5 stars
Five Stars
I loved this book. The flow of the story was great with interesting characters.
5.0 out of 5 stars

Five Stars
Loved this story. Great flow, interesting characters. Should you read this, yes you should.
I can't wait for part 2.

5.0 out of 5 stars
I really enjoyed it!
Started reading and could not put it down. I really enjoyed it!!

4.0 out of 5 stars
This book and story are not my normal genre so I was initially hesitant. Once I started reading, I was totally caught up in the story and the characters. I would recommend this to all of my friends that are interested in a great story of personal tragedy and personal resolve to overcome great lose.

Five Stars
This was an excellent book and it kept me guessing about what was coming – next on every page! In fact... I was a little upset that I got to the last page so quickly!! :-) I loved how the lives of each character all messed together. This book was a wonderful book to read. The writing was excellent and the "language" outstanding. It told a great story about surviving life's difficult moments.

Library of Congress Control Number (LCCN): 2018903432

Fiction: Contemporary

ISBN: 978-0-9973475-1-7

Published by Joyce Smith Printed in the USA, First Edition - Paperback and Electronic

ACKNOWLEDGEMENTS

I give honor and glory to the Almighty for keeping me on course. It took encouragement for me to complete this book. I thank my husband, Andre Smith, for reading my book, making corrections, and for his support. I thank my son, Charles Turner, III, grandchildren, siblings, and all other family members and friends for their support.

Special thanks to Dorothy J Morris, author of "The Fatal Trilogy," for editing my book, and Nikkea Sharee, author of "They Call Me Crazy," for proofreading. I am also very thankful to my other readers: Stella Adams, author of "Heavy Is the Rain," Angelina Sills, Earlene Whitworth Hill," Phyllis Greene, and Marquita Hill.

Thank you to James Jones, of Jimi Jones Visual for the book cover.

To those who purchase this book, thank you. As with "Cuts Like A Knife," may "Cuts To The Soul," inspire hope and community participation in my beloved City of Baltimore.

I dedicate this book to my mother, Marion Smith and grandmother, Hazel Harriday. They will forever be in my heart.

CHAPTER 1

Eric's Place, named after Walter Jones' deceased grandson was having its opening today on the sixth anniversary of his death. As Walter drove pass the announcement, he considered if he should go to work or attend the ceremony.

Squinting at the sunlight bouncing off the sign, Walter thought how the money he earned if he went to work would not help his finances. His girlfriend, Brenda's out-of-control spending was the reason the two of them lived for several years with Curtis and Nicky, his brother, and sister-in-law.

Why waste this beautiful sunny day at work he wondered, deciding to attend the opening. Walter made a turn at the next corner. He drove toward his home, figuring he had time to rest and change out of his work uniform before the event started.

Unlocking the front door, Walter entered the small two-story row house in west Baltimore. The constant hum of the refrigerator and drips from the water faucet in the meticulous kitchen were the only sounds he heard. Nicky would have been home drinking coffee, listening to her gospels, and fixing breakfast; but she left last night to go on a weekend church revival.

Walter climbed the stairs to the second floor and heard a loud moan. He stopped when he heard the sound again—this time louder. Curtis did not go with Nicky to the revival and claimed he was sick. Walter thought his brother was just finding an excuse not to attend the event, but the moans gave him concern.

The groan of a familiar woman's voice caused the younger brother to realize he heard sounds of sex, not distress. The grunts and shrieks became rapid, loud, and vulgar, almost drowning out the thumps of his beating heart. Walter ran up the stairs to Curtis and Nicky's bedroom, kicked the door open, and froze as he found his so-called sick brother and Brenda in the bed naked.

"Oh my God," Curtis screamed as he jumped up and retrieved his underwear from the floor. "I'm so sorry Walt." Sweat dripped down Curtis' face as he rushed to his brother still standing at the door,

"I... didn't mean for you... to see this."

Brenda wrapped the bed sheet around her ample breast and shapely body as she hurried to Walter. "He forced me, and said I owed him sex since I'm living in his house."

"That's a lie Walt," Curtis pleaded to his brother.

"He told me he couldn't get anything this good from that holier-than-thou wife of his," Brenda pouted.

"You lying bitch! Keep your foul mouth off my wife," Curtis screamed as he pushed his brother's girlfriend.

Brenda fell back against the wall, the sheet slid from her body as she slipped to the floor with her head tilted forward.

Walter growled standing over her, "Get your stinky ass up, drama queen." He saw a blood smear on the wall and blood dripping from the steel hook holding a plaque. Walter poked Brenda's arm, and she fell over on her side. He turned to his brother, yelled and pointed, "She must've hit her head on that steel hook holding your stupid old football emblem. What have you done?"

Checking Brenda's wrist for a pulse, and not finding one, Walter performed chest compressions and breathed into her mouth. Blood seeped out of the back of her head, spilling onto the green, gray, and pink linoleum floor. Walter continued trying to revive Brenda's limp body. He checked again, but still did not find a pulse. "She's dead," he mumbled in a shaky voice.

Curtis dropped to the floor on his knees yelling at Brenda's still body, "Woman, get up!" He shook her, and she moved like a rag doll. "It was an awful accident Walt," he shrieked turning to his brother. "You know it was an accident."

Walter blinked back tears and muttered, "We should call the police."

"Please Walt. I'll go to jail," Curtis begged, grabbing his brother's hand. "I'm a sick man and got sugar real bad," he replied with tears falling from his eyes.

"Your diabetes didn't keep you from screwing her." Walter snatched his hand from his brother.

Curtis cried still dressed in his underwear, "I made a terrible mistake. Please forgive me," he pleaded.

Trembling as his brother cried, Walter noticed how thin and fragile Curtis appeared. "What now?" Walter asked.

Curtis dried his eyes with the back of his hand. "I have a large piece of tarp in the basement from when I painted houses," he offered out of breath. "We can wrap her in it."

"Cover her in a piece of tarp." Walter frowned, "Then what?"

"Stay here. I'll explain everything when I get back."

Curtis put on his shirt and pants and left the room. Walter sat on the floor beside his deceased girlfriend and stared into the mirror located over the black lacquered dresser. His reflection showed black wavy hair with more sprinkles of gray than he recalled. His wooing bedroom eyes now came with bags under them, and his once proud six-pack had vanished into a full stomach. Walter wondered if the changes he saw in his appearance were from time, Brenda's insanity, or both.

Resting his head on his knees, he stared at her still nude body with what appeared to be a smirk on her face. "Even dead you torment me. Why did I stay with you? You stole my life." Walter grabbed his head knowing his deceased girlfriend had not stolen his life, but he had given it away to her. He once found her exciting. Brenda was fun and loved to party. Walter enjoyed her carefree attitude, but soon their lifestyle got old.

He banged his fist on the floor, and shouted at her, "You wanted the good things in life: cars, clothes, and jewelry; but you didn't want to work hard for them. Did you?" Walter thought about how Brenda went to social affairs and flea markets selling clothes, jewelry, and cosmetics. He figured she could not have made any money as she always complained about being broke and grumbled over living with his family. "You were her fool," he told his reflection.

Interrupting Walter's thoughts, Curtis reentered the room with a large piece of tarp, a bucket of water, a bottle of ammonia, cords, and two dry cloths. Sweating and breathing hard, he laid out the tarp next to Brenda's body. "Help me roll her onto it. Hold her while I tie the ends."

Walter grabbed his stomach and held his hand to his mouth, "Curtis, I'm feeling sick."

"Not now, Walt. I don't need you wimping out on me."

"You can't put this on me," Walter shouted, pointing his finger at his brother. "Why'd you have to sleep with her?"

"She kept coming after me. When Brenda climbed into my bed this morning, I gave in." Curtis held his brother by the shoulders. "There's no excuse for what I've done, but in the forty years Nicky and I've been married, I was not unfaithful... until today."

"I wish you had said something," Walter pulled away from his brother.

"Tell me what I should've said?" Curtis hung his head. "I guess I could've told you the woman you've spent a good part of your life with and who treated you like a dog was trying to screw me?"

"Yes, if you couldn't find another way."

Curtis continued to tie a cord around the tarp holding Brenda's body. "Should I've included how you took up with her while your child's mother was fighting for her life?"

"Trust me, I regret sleeping with Brenda while Linda was dying," Walter cried, "I've been a fool and have nothing to show for my life." He clutched his head and stammered, "My daughter doesn't even know me. I left Asia with Mike and Pearl when she was only twelve and grieving for her mother." Walter dropped his head and exhaled, "I'm a grown man living with my brother like a teenager."

"They may have been identical twin sisters, but Linda was a good woman. How you'd go from her to Brenda, and stay for nineteen years, is beyond me." Curtis scratched his head. "But your life's not over and punishing ourselves is a waste of time. Help me cleanup this blood." Curtis added some ammonia to the water, gave one cloth to Walter and dipped the other in the bucket, wrung it, and wiped away the blood from the wall. "Who knows why Brenda did anything? Maybe she slept with me to hurt you."

Curtis replaced the cloth in the bucket, wrung it again, and continued to clean the wall. "She hated Nicky. She might have done it to hurt my wife, or because she could." He shook his head. "Either way don't matter."

Walter shrugged his shoulders, hung his head, and dabbed a tear sliding down his face. "You might be right," Walter agreed while cleaning blood from the floor. "But what we gonna do with her body?"

"I promised Nicky you'd help me plant rose bushes in the back yard today."

"How'd you promise that?"

Ignoring Walter's question Curtis instructed, "I have a bag of limestone in the basement we can pour over Brenda's body to absorb the odor and place the rose bushes on top of her." Curtis paced back and forth. "She's a small woman. Nobody gonna pay any attention. It'll look like we're just planting bushes."

"That's a crazy idea."

"Please Walt, I know it will work. Besides, if I hadn't been trying to help you out, I wouldn't be in this jam," he stuttered. "I was weak, but I can't go to jail."

Walter shook his head. "What makes you think no one will see us burying a body?"

"Hell, you can shoot somebody round here in the middle of the day in front of a hundred people, and nobody notices." Curtis finished tying the tarp. "It's hard and I'm sorry, but I need you to be strong."

"I'll do my best," Walter sighed. "But now I don't owe you nothing... nothing at all."

CHAPTER 2

"Leave her body against the back door for now," Curtis said out of breath, as he and Walter dragged Brenda down the stairs to the rear of the house. "The bushes are against the house on my wagon," Curtis instructed.

"Where in the yard are we burying... planting the bushes?" Walter inquired.

Curtis looked around the yard. "Nicky wanted them near the house, but we'll plant them at the end of the yard. The house across the alley is vacant, so there's less chance people will see us."

"Won't Nicky be upset?"

"No, she'll be glad we planted them. My wife's easy to please."

"Yes, she is. Too bad you forgot that today."

Curtis frowned and sighed, "Let's just get busy before my neighbors come out."

"I'm not sure it's a good idea, burying the body in the backyard." Walter stood at the back door looking at Brenda's tarp-wrapped body. "Why don't we wait until tonight and dump her in Leakin Park?"

Curtis shook his head, "Bodies get discovered there by people all the time. A jogger or somebody walking their dog could stumble over her."

"Not if we take her deep into the woods."

"No guarantee. People go deep in the woods to dump bodies." Curtis cocked his head to the side, "How many bodies have been found there?"

Walter shrugged. "Why can't we drive to the shore?"

"Even if we do, we have to rent a boat, and still a fisherman could hook her body." Curtis shook his head again, "No, this way nobody will stumble over her. The limestone should keep small animals or rodents from digging in the yard."

"It's so creepy, every time I look out the rear window or go in the backyard I'll think of her being buried there."

"How often have you gone in the backyard since you've lived here or looked out the rear windows?" Curtis took his brother's hand, "No matter where we bury or dump her, it won't erase the memory."

The older brother pulled a red wagon to the rear door. "This way we know where she is at all times." Explaining, he continued pulling the wagon. "Me and my wife been here over thirty-five years and ain't going nowhere." Curtis gestured for his brother to help him place the body on the wagon. "If there's a problem, we'll know right away."

Walter sighed, "You're right, it's so hard."

"Man, you were with this woman for nineteen years. You must've had feelings for her. Heck, if not, you're right about wasting your life." Curtis patted his brother on the back. "Trust me, we'll get through this."

They moved the wagon to the end of the yard, dug a deep trench, and put Brenda's body in the hole. The two men threw limestone over her before planting the bushes on top. After they finished, Curtis and Walter placed the two shovels on the wagon and pushed it against the back wall of the house.

"Want me to take the shovels to the basement?" Walter asked wiping sweat from his forehead.

"Yeah, and while you're there bring up two of Brenda's suitcases." Curtis went into the house and flopped into a chair at the kitchen table. "I'm not feeling well and need to eat."

"Stay here and I'll fix something after I take the shovels down to the basement and bring up the suitcases," Walter offered following Curtis into the kitchen. "Why am I bringing up the suitcases?"

"I'll tell you when you get back?"

Walter placed the shovels on marked hooks in the basement and retrieved Brenda's suitcases from the crawlspace under the steps.

When he returned to the kitchen, Curtis was drinking a glass of orange juice. "What you want to eat?"

"Just fix eggs and toast. I'm not real hungry but have to watch my blood sugar."

"I'll fix them for both of us. I never cooked in this kitchen before, but everything's so organized. I shouldn't have a problem."

"You sure didn't," Curtis grumbled as he placed his glass on the brown wooden table, "and neither had your girlfriend."

"I'm... sorry," Walter stammered.

"Y'all acted as if you were in a hotel." Curtis finished drinking his orange juice. "Don't get me wrong, we appreciated the rent, but a helping hand would've been real nice." Curtis took his glass and placed it in the sink. "My wife cooked and cleaned the entire time you two were here and neither of you ever offered to help her."

"I've been so selfish, but I... promise I'll make everything up to you and Nicky."

"Let's concentrate on getting through this for right now. We still got a lot to do if we're gonna pull this thing off."

"Like what?"

"We gotta say something happened to Brenda. She didn't disappear into thin air."

"Huh?"

"Need to make it seem as if she left on her own. That's why I asked you to bring up her suitcases." Curtis paused, "I need you to dress as Brenda, put on one of her wigs, and drive her car."

"Curtis you've lost your mind!"

"No I haven't—thinking real clear. I'm too tall, but you could pull it off."

Walter took the eggs out of the refrigerator while complaining, "I'm also taller than her."

"Brenda wore heels, which made her seem taller. You're shorter, and closer to her complexion. I'm too dark."

"Really, I'm just gonna put on Brenda's wig and pretend I'm her." Walter grunted, "That's crazy. No one will buy it."

"We'll wait till it gets dark. Some face powder, bright red lipstick, her blond wig, and a flashy top; trust me, no one will know the difference."

Walter placed scrambled eggs and toast in front of Curtis. "Suppose this works and everyone thinks I'm Brenda, then what?"

"I'll put the suitcases in her trunk. I don't want to give anyone time to get a good look at you. After I put the bags in the trunk, jump in, and drive away." Curtis stopped talking and exhaled. "Go to Aunt Daisy's, and park in her backyard."

"Won't she think its strange Brenda is parking her car in the yard?"

"I'll call and tell her you're parking the car cause it got traffic violations." Curtis turned to his brother, "Take the wig off before you get there, and don't forget to make sure she hears your voice if you don't want to get shot."

"Yeah between her dementia, poor hearing, and sight loss I got to always be careful around her."

Curtis rolled his eyes and pointed his finger at Walter, "You'll be old one day."

"Sorry, you're right, but we can't leave the car in her yard forever."

"Don't worry; I'll have it worked out by tonight."

"Good, I'm going to the grand opening of Eric's Place today."

After Walter left, Curtis opened his wallet and pulled out several pieces of folded paper. He opened each one and continued searching until he found what he wanted. He used the house phone to make a call. "Let me speak to Lil Moe," he requested.

"Yeah, who's this?"

"Is this Moe?"

"Who's asking?"

"Man, it's Curt."

"Hey buddy. Had any problems with your car?"

"Nah, you did a good job. I'm calling bout something else."

"Huh?"

"You still junk cars, don't you?"

"Trying to get rid of something?"

"Yeah: a 97 Camry."

"Why you want to scrap a car that's only five-years old?"

"It's been having transmission problems and my brother's tired of fixing it. He wants to get rid of it."

"You should've brought it to me."

"I told him to, but family never listens." Curtis used his hand to wipe sweat from his forehead. "You interested?"

"Sure, I can pick it up Monday."

"Good, it'll be parked behind my aunt's house on Park Heights."

CHAPTER 3

Eric's Place was once a barbershop where Asia sat on the floor holding and rocking her precious child killed by a stray bullet. Now, six years later the building was a youth center where children could learn and feel safe. The shop was narrow but deep. Asia had some interior walls removed, providing open working spaces. She converted the second floor into her office, a bathroom, and arts and craft rooms.

The original plan was to open Eric's Place for boys, but the women in the community argued for girls to be included.

Asia's heart swelled as she sat in a chair looking at her son's picture surrounded by blue and white balloons. His small brown face with his twinkling eyes and crooked little smile cut her heart like a knife. It would be several hours before the festivities started, but she needed this quiet time alone.

"It's happening today sweetheart," Asia uttered, embracing the picture. She recalled how once after Eric died, she heard her son's voice. Aunt Pearl, who helped raise Asia after her mother's death, said Eric would always be a part of his mother.

Asia bowed her head, and gave thanks for the opening celebration. She prayed for help to get through the day, and caressed her stomach as Ericka, her unborn daughter kicked.

The young woman lifted her head and saw Uncle Mike approaching. She went to the door and unlocked it to let him into the center. She was grateful for her uncle who filled the void left by her neglectful father.

"Where's your husband, Winston Augustus? We're supposed to meet at 1:00." Mike hugged her. "The opening begins in two hours, and Pearl will be here soon with the caterers."

"He's on his way. We don't live across the street, and every time you call him by his full name, I crack-up."

"At least everyone knows who I'm talking about. Patty calls him Winston and you call him Augustus. Heck, half the time I didn't know who you all were talking about." Mike chuckled, "See, when I call his name, nobody's confused."

"Uncle Mike, I love you so very much," Asia wrapped her arms around her uncle's neck as her husband and stepson came to the door.

"I love you more and don't you forget it." Mike kissed Asia on her forehead and directed his attention to the man and boy as he opened the door to let them into the center. "Bout time you guys got here," he said smiling. "I thought I'd have to set-up the chairs by myself."

"You know I wouldn't let you down Uncle Mike." Win said brushing his blond hair out of his blue eyes, looking like a younger version of his father. "Dad's the slacker."

"Where's your loyalty boy?" Augustus came back playfully tapping his son on the head.

Asia enjoyed listening to the three males interact with each other as they arranged chairs and reflected on how difficult the past six years since her son's death had been. Graduating from college with a degree in elementary education and attaining a teaching job were demanding, but not as difficult as starting Eric's Place.

The project almost did not happen until Augustus received a partnership agreement from the university where he was the head of the science department. Patty swayed her husband, Dr. John Drake, to obtain a sizeable endowment from the hospital where he was a chief surgeon. There were problems with zoning, permits, and other issues, and Asia believed she could not have opened the center without her friends and family.

"Man you've been here for several years, its 2002, time to give up the Patriots." Mike scolded Asia's husband.

"The Ravens haven't proven themselves yet," Augustus defended.

"Dad, the team's only six years old."

"That's right Win, and already they've won an AFC title," Mike bragged.

Asia was pleased her uncle and husband were now friends. Mike was skeptical of Augustus when they first met.

Her mind drifted back to the first time she met the man who became her husband. After Eric died, Patty took Asia to meet her friend, Winston Augustus. His wife had passed away less than a year earlier and the family was still grieving. Win was the most serious seven-year old Asia had met. He guarded his gregarious, redheaded, freckled-face, four-year-old sister, Lizzie like a ninja warrior.

During the visit in Boston, Patty's friend was so impressed with Asia; he offered her a job as a nanny to his children. She planned to accept the position, but later declined. Asia decided instead to open Eric's Place in her hometown.

Although, Asia did not accepting the position as a nanny to Augustus' children, he still became one of her biggest cheerleaders and encouragers. Nevertheless, she wondered how much he cared. Augustus did not ask Asia on a date until her graduation day.

Together, they built a strong-trusting bond before marriage. Waiting, gave Asia the time she needed to develop and become a mature woman. It also helped prepare them for the trials of a multiracial-blended family.

***

Walter entered and sat at the rear of the center. He caught his daughter's eye and waved as she grimaced. Mike turned around, saw his niece's father, frowned, and whispered to the man next to him. Walter wondered if the man was Asia's husband, since he did not receive an invitation to his daughter's wedding. It also hurt knowing Mike walked her down the aisle.

Asia's father did not receive an invitation to the grand opening of Eric's Place. He found out from a neighbor and saw the sign of the event when driving by the building this morning.

Walter's daughter was more beautiful than the last time he saw her six years ago at Eric's funeral. Although, it was a tough time for his daughter, he was still not a comfort to her. Dropping his head, Walter had to admit his own actions caused this treatment from Asia.

Observing Asia's stomach, Walter wondered how many more months it might be before this grandchild entered the world. He looked at the picture of Eric with regret and hoped he would get to know this child.

Asia was giving her concluding remarks, but Walter's mind focused on the awful events that happened several hours before he came to the celebration. Walter had blood on his hands. He hoped his daughter never found out about his involvement in Brenda's death. Walter quietly left after Asia finished her comments, vowing to reach out to her soon.

CHAPTER 4

Walter returned home after the ceremony at Eric's Place ended to find Curtis sitting at the kitchen table writing notes on a pad.

"I've got the car situation figured out," Curtis said to Walter as he entered the kitchen. "I've been real busy since you left," the older brother made check marks on his paper. "Packed several bags of Brenda's clothes and shoes, and threw them away at dumpsters around the city." He made more notes on his pad. "It makes it look as if she's gone, in case anyone checks your closet." Curtis stopped writing and looked at his brother, "You can now take your clothes out of the trash bags you keep them in." He shook his head. "Now, you can put them in the empty drawers and the closet." Curtis frowned, "How could one woman have so many pairs of shoes?"

"What about the car?" Walter asked irritated. He knew Curtis was being thorough, but still resented the comment about how his clothes were in garbage bags, although it was true.

"A friend of mine is picking it up Monday and... junking it."

"What! Are you serious? The car's only five-years old, paid for, and worth much more than we can get for scraping it."

"You wanna put an ad in the newspaper? This not gonna be easy. We've got to make a few sacrifices."

"You mean I have to make sacrifices."

"Don't start whining Walt. After you drop off the car, remove the tags and clean out the inside and the trunk."

"Why not just keep the car?"

"No one will believe Brenda left without taking her car." Curtis made another check on the paper. "How was the celebration?"

"Impressive. There were lots of people there, and the Mayor gave Asia an award for her hard work." Walter exhaled, "It's a shame an innocent child died before anybody does anything round here."

"You act surprised."

"No, just tired of the violence. I'm going to ask Asia if I can volunteer at the center."

Curtis smiled, "That's a good idea. Hope it works."

Walter shook his head frowning, "I left right after the celebration ended, wasn't ready to deal with Mike."

Sighing Curtis reminded his brother, "You'll have to deal with him one day." He closed his pad. "I'm going upstairs to rest. It'll be dark in a few hours, and then the real work starts."

***

Curtis entered his bedroom and fell across the bed. His body and head ached. One slip, he thought, and my whole life's in jeopardy. "It's not fair," he screamed at the ceiling. He was afraid someone would find out about Brenda, and he could go to jail, or lose Nicky. "I rather die than hurt Nicky," he said as he raised his head and look at his reflection in the mirror.

He continued staring at himself as he admitted enjoying the advances Brenda made to him. She was an attractive woman, and it had been a long time since he received attention from a woman other than his wife. "That should've been enough," he yelled scolding his reflection.

"Why did I do it?" he asked aloud staring at the deep lines around his mouth and eyes. "I didn't even like the woman." He shook his head, "I hated the way she treated my brother and my wife." He again pointed his finger at his reflection and asked, "Am I that starved for attention?"

Despite his fear, Curtis put on a front. There were only three years between him and his brother, but he had always taken care of Walter.

Their mother often admonished Curtis as a child to look out for his younger brother. "He's your little brother and is not as strong as you," she would tell Curtis. The older brother thought about his mother as he left his bed and removed the steel bracket from the wall. He could hear her say, "You're locking the front door after the crooks have stolen all your furniture." His mother had a saying for every situation. She would be very disappointed in him he thought, but not as much as he was in himself.

Nicky asked him numerous times to remove the bracket and put his plaque in the living room on the mantle, but he liked waking up every day looking at it. Reminded him of when he was somebody. If he had done as Nicky asked, Brenda would still be alive. He had to remind himself she would also be alive if he had not slept with her.

The pain in Curtis' head increased, he returned to the bed, and closed his eyes. When he opened them, Brenda was standing over him with a mixture of limestone, twigs, and mud in her hair and covering her nude body. Her eyes were large black holes in her head, and her toothless mouth twisted to the side of her face.

"You didn't like my sweet honey?" she asked holding out her muddy hands.

Curtis jumped up with his heart pounding and his shaking body, soaking wet. He realized he had fallen asleep and was having an awful nightmare. It was dark; he retrieved his flashlight from the dresser in his bedroom, opened the window, and pointed the beam at the place in the yard where he and Walter buried Brenda's body. He could see from the light, the bushes had not been disturbed.

***

Walter entered the living room after Curtis went upstairs thinking how right his brother was about him and Brenda acting as if they were in a hotel. They spent most of their time in their bedroom watching TV, coming out when Nicky called them to eat.

He picked up a framed photograph of Nicky and Curtis when they first married, and were young and beautiful. Curtis did not age as well as Nicky. She had not changed much over the years: a little heavier, hair thinned and grayed, and light laugh lines around her eyes in her light brown face. However, her beautiful smile could still lighten a dark room.

Walter walked over to the mantel and retrieved an old high school photograph of Curtis, Mike, and their teammates in football uniforms. His brother had promise, but all hopes of going pro ended when Curtis injured his knee, leaving him with a slight limp. Walter recalled how the girls followed his brother around school before he was hurt; but after his injury, the only one still there was Nicky.

Returning to the mantle, he stared at a photograph of Mike and Curtis. They had their arms around each other and were best friends. They continued to be close until he became involved with Brenda. Walter agonized over how many people he and his girlfriend hurt. Even when he started seeing Brenda in public, Curtis continued to protect him against Mike and the many other critics.

Walter sat back in the chair and closed his eyes, regretting the years he spent with Brenda. The image of his girlfriend's dead nude body haunted him. *This is crazy. I can't do it.* He wished he had gone to work this morning.

"Curtis wouldn't be in this position if it hadn't been for me," Walter mumbled with his head in his hands. He was sorry he had not been a better man and father. For years, Walter blamed his behavior on grief, Mike, or whatever excuse he could conceive. "What a mess I've made," Walter cried. "God please forgive me," he prayed drifting off to sleep in the chair.

CHAPTER 5

Curtis entered the living room, turned on the lamp, and watched Walter twist and turn as he slept.

"Walt, wake up," Curtis leaned over and shook his brother's arm, "It's time to get started."

"I can't believe it's dark already. I just closed my eyes," Walter yawed.

"It's nice outside, about 78 degrees with a slight summer night's breeze." Curtis walked over and looked through the screen in the open window. "Several people are sitting on their front steps, and I hear a radio playing... perfect." Curtis sat on the edge of the sofa and looked Walter in the eyes. "I know this has been difficult, but we're almost home. Tonight's important." He patted his brother on his knee. "We have to convince those people out there sitting on their front steps you're Brenda."

"I'm good," Walter exhaled and stammered. "I can do this."

Curtis nodded to his brother, "Kept Brenda's makeup kit, and her blond wig. Need you to shave before putting on the makeup." He hesitated before adding, "Your mustache too."

"Not my mustache! I'll only be out there for a few seconds. It'll be dark, and as you said no one will get a real peek at me."

"It won't be pitch black, there're several streetlights. I'm not asking you to slit your throat."

"Don't know how much more of this I can take." Walter placed his head in his hands.

"This is it. After tonight, we're home free little brother."

The two men reviewed the plans several times, and Walter went into the bathroom to shave and dress. He stared at himself in the mirror, took a deep breath, and shaved his face including his mustache. He felt his stomach rumbling and grabbed the sides of the sink.

"This is it, we're almost there," he told his reflection. He smoothed foundation and powder over his face and applied bright red lipstick. He put on the long blond wig. Looked into the mirror and saw Brenda staring back at him. He grabbed the wig off his head and fell to the floor. Walter had trouble breathing, as sweat poured down his face ruining his makeup.

Curtis knocked on the bathroom door, "Walt you okay in there?"

"Yeah, give me a minute. This putting on makeup is not as easy as it looks," he laughed trying to sound normal.

"I can help you."

"No, I'm good, thanks."

Walter sat on the closed toilet seat. *I have to do this.* He returned to the mirror and reapplied the face powder. His hands were shaking so bad, he had to continue wiping the lipstick from his face as he kept missing his lips. Satisfied he had done his best, Walter walked out to meet his brother.

"Man, this will definitely work. You almost fooled me." Curtis inspected Walter as he left the bathroom. "Since Brenda blouses were too small, wear this large shiny necklace over your tee shirt. I saved it when I packed her clothes."

Curtis fastened the necklace around his brother's neck. "You're shaking, and your neck is soaking wet. Let's sit in the kitchen for a few minutes."

"Suppose this don't work?" Walter asked, his voice trembling.

"It'll work. All you need to do is jump in the car and pull off. Nobody will have any reason not to believe you're Brenda." Curtis put his hands on his brother's shoulder. "You did a real good job on the makeup, and the wig is what will catch most people's attention."

"Yeah, you're right, I'm just nervous."

"I understand and it's normal," Curtis smiled at his brother. "It's show time Walt. You wait in the vestibule until I place the bags in the trunk."

Curtis left the house with two of Brenda's suitcases, banging them against the steps as he carried them, fussing, and cursing loud enough for anyone nearby to hear. He placed the suitcases into the trunk and slammed the lid. He reentered the house, gave his brother the car keys, and nudged him down the stairs. Walter stumbled, ran to the car, jumped in, and sped away.

After the car left, Curtis looked around to insure he had his neighbors' full attention. He waved his hand and shouted as the car left. "Good riddance. I'm glad that bitch is gone," he shouted walking back and forth performing. "She treated my brother like shit; all he did was work to please her. I hope she never comes back."

CHAPTER 6

For over two hours, Marie Zackey sat in the train station in Baltimore on the hard, old, wooden bench waiting for her mother. She watched people as they caught or disembarked from their trains. She wondered what she would do if her mother never appeared.

Marie could not return to her home in Philadelphia. She quit her job, turned in the keys to the apartment she shared with her late aunt, and sold or gave away most of their belongings. All she had left was in her small suitcase and tote bag. Marie's stomach growled. She dialed her mother's number again and listened to her call go straight to voice mail. Her mother claimed she had placed a deposit on a house and stashed away twenty-thousand dollars. Since Marie's father was coming home from prison after twenty years, the money would allow the three of them to make a new start. The young woman could not resist her mother's offer as she had her own plans for the money.

Marie's head pounded with pain as her stomach churned. She was hungry but did not want to chance missing her mother while she went to the canteen or the restroom.

She wished her father's sister were still alive. Aunt Tissy would know what to do, she thought as she retrieved a piece of paper out of her wallet. She remembered Aunt Tissy telling her before she died, "Put this paper in your wallet. Here's the name and address of your mother's brother." Marie smoothed the creases on the paper. "Go there if you have a real emergency." I guess this qualifies, she thought.

The station security guard came by for the third time asking if she was okay.

"Sir, can you tell me where this address is located?" she responded to his inquiry.

The pudgy guard took the paper from her and looked at it over his glasses. "Yeah it's real close only about ten or fifteen minutes from here."

"Please tell me how to get a cab?"

"They're right outside the door. I was real worried about you." He returned the paper to Marie. "You should've told me where you wanted to go."

"I was waiting for someone, but thanks I'll be leaving now."

"Sure, just be careful."

Marie pulled her suitcase and placed her tote bag over her shoulder. There were yellow taxis lined-up in front of the station. She was glad, as it was getting dark.

She got into the first cab, gave the driver the address on Lafayette Avenue, and sat back trying to calm her nerves. It was a short ride as the guard said it would be. The driver stopped in front of a large stone house with marble steps and stained glass windows in the door and at the top of the front windows.

She paid him, removed her bags, and left the cab. Walking up the front steps, she stopped and turned to ask the driver to wait, but it was too late as she watched him pull away.

Marie rang the bell and a little girl with red hair and freckles answered the door. "What do you want?" the child asked.

"I like to speak to Michael Wallace," Marie answered, wondering if this was the right house and wishing she had asked the taxi driver to wait before she got out of the cab.

"Uncle Mike somebody wants you," the girl hollered leaving the front door open.

Marie could only see into the vestibule, but heard voices and music. She wondered if she was interrupting something.

A tall man with gray hair, hazel-colored eyes, and deep brown skin coloring came to the door.

"How may I help you?" he asked in a deep voice blocking the entrance to the house.

"Are you Michael Wallace?"

"Who are you?"

"My name is Marie, and I'm looking for my mother, Brenda Zackey," the young woman stammered.

38

"I've a sister named Brenda Wallace not Zackey, but I haven't seen her in years. She couldn't be your mother."

A woman reached around Mike and took Marie's hand. "My name is Pearl come in honey. Mike get her suitcase."

Marie entered the home and realized she was interrupting a party. There were at least twenty pairs of eyes on her.

"Brenda couldn't be your mother," the man repeated. "And if so, why come here looking for her?"

"I came here from Philly, and my mother was supposed to pick me up from the train station but she didn't show. My Aunt Tissy gave me your address." Marie looked around the room trying to avoid the stares. She noticed a picture of a little boy, and her mother on the mantle over the fireplace. "You have a picture of my mother on your mantle," she said pointing her finger.

"That's my mother," a voice said appearing into the room.

This must be the famous Asia, Marie thought. Brenda told her about the older cousin, how everyone was always concerned about Asia's welfare. Even more so, after her mother and later son died. Now, Asia was a super star who saved the children in the area. Marie and her cousin favored, with their deep brown skin tones and hazel colored eyes. The biggest difference between them other than their ages was Marie had about twenty pounds on her willowy pregnant cousin. The younger cousin wished she had experienced some of the concern and support Asia enjoyed over the years.

"That's right your mother and mine were identical twins, and I'm named after our late grandmother," Marie smiled. "Did I interrupt a party?" she asked noticing people leaving.

"No, it's late. We had the celebration of Eric's Place today named after Asia's son." Pearl took the picture from the mantel and gave it to Marie. "Are you hungry? Would you like something to eat?"

"Yes please. I haven't eaten since this morning," Marie smiled.

"After everyone leaves and you finish eating, we've got some talking to do." Mike directed the visitor toward the kitchen.

Marie followed her uncle through the house, and admired the beauty of the home with its chandeliers and as her Aunt Tissy used to say, "Real hardwood floors."

Pearl fixed a plate of food, placed it into the microwave, and after a few minutes put it in front of their guest. Marie smiled and accepted the food. She liked this woman with her smooth, pecan-colored face and kind, sweet demeanor. Mike and Asia sat staring at her as she ate.

"How old are you? And where've you been all these years we never met you?" Mike asked not allowing Marie to finish her food.

"I'm twenty-one and lived with my father's sister, Aunt Tissy and her husband, Uncle Hank in Hunting Park until he died several years ago." Marie took a few more bites of her food, "Then me and my aunt moved into an apartment."

"How do we know you're Brenda's child?"

"Mike, let's not jump to conclusions." Pearl reached across the table and patted his hand.

"I'm serious Pearl. A grown woman walks in here and says she's Brenda's child. What do you want, Marie?"

"I'm only trying to find my mother. We're getting a place together. Wait, let me get my bag." Marie left the table and retrieved her tote bag from the living room. She reentered the kitchen, removed a picture of a house, and a small photo album.

"My birth certificate shouldn't be hard to get. Meanwhile, look at the picture of the house my mother said she put a deposit on and my photo album." She gave them to Mike. "In the album are pictures of my mother, aunt, and uncle at various stages in my life." Marie walked around the table and pointed out different photographs. "This is my first Christmas. I was eleven on this picture of me and my mother when I won the spelling bee in the sixth grade."

Marie returned to her seat as Mike looked at her photographs. He stopped when he got to the last picture. "Who's this man with my sister holding a baby?"

"That's me as a baby with my mother and father."

"What's his name?"

"Uh... Leroy Zackey," Marie answered with hesitation, seeing the strange expression on Mike's face.

"Oh my God, Big Zack is your father. No wonder Brenda kept it a secret," Mike answered placing his head into his hands. "How often do you see him?"

"I haven't seen him since I was a little girl." Marie hung her head. "It may have been too hard for my aunt or mother to take me since I lived in another state...."

"You must be tired honey," Pearl asked interrupting Marie. "Would you like to stay the night?"

Marie smiled at Pearl, "I'm worn out, but I don't want to be a bother. I never imagined Brenda wouldn't have met me at the train station."

"No bother at all. We'd love to have you. Wouldn't we Mike?"

Pearl's husband looked at Asia and mumbled, "Yeah, she can stay."

"Good, grab her bag Mike."

Asia remained in the kitchen, waiting for her aunt and uncle to return. After Marie crashed their gathering, she asked her husband to take the kids and go home while she tried to find out more about her newfound cousin. She did not say anything while her uncle was questioning Marie, but had a bad feeling about the young woman.

"Want something to drink," Mike offered as he returned to the kitchen interrupting Asia's thoughts.

"No thanks. What's your take on her?"

"I don't know, but I'm calling Ray to ask him to check on her and Zackey." Mike placed his hand on Asia's shoulder. "Don't you worry about this sweetheart."

"I won't Uncle Mike, but something doesn't seem right. I'm going home, but call me if you find out anything."

CHAPTER 7

Arriving at his aunt's backyard, Curtis saw a figure sitting in Brenda's car, and hoped it was Walter. The inside light flashed on his brother's face as Curtis opened the front door on the passenger's side of the car. He wondered why Walter did not go inside their aunt's house.

"Man, you look like a cross between a clown and a serial killer. You've smeared make-up and lipstick all over your face." Cracking a smile, Curtis attempted not to laugh.

"I tried to wipe the make-up off with a paper towel."

"Wait, Nicky has wet wipes in the car. Good thing you didn't go in the house, you would've scared our aunt to death. She's not that blind."

"I didn't see a light on, and figured she was sleep. Aunt Daisy never seemed to care for me, anyway."

"Come-on Walt, she's old, got problems with her memory, hearing, and sight. She sure ain't got time for your bull-shit." Curtis gave Walter the pack of wipes, and retrieved them after his brother removed several. "She's been there for us, and you owe her respect. You get everything out the car?"

"Yes, good grief."

"Calm down and let's go home."

After a short quiet ride from their aunt's house, Curtis pulled up and parked his car in front of his door. "Walt, it's over, and you did real good."

The phone rang as the two men entered their home, and they both froze.

"Answer... it's your house," Walter stated.

"Right, it might be Nicky."

Curtis could not contain his surprise. Mike was on the phone, and the older brother missed the old friendship the two of them once shared. The only other time Mike called since Walter and Brenda started seeing each other was when Eric died.

"Is Brenda there? She's not answering her cell phone." Mike asked.

"No... she stormed out of here, threw two of suitcases in her car, and sped off about an hour ago. Sure you got the right number?" Curtis asked, rubbing his forehead.

"I think so. I got it from her daughter."

"Who'd you say?

"A woman claiming to be Brenda's daughter showed up a couple of hours ago. It's my first time meeting her. Is Walter there?"

"Walt wasn't home when Brenda left. He's at our aunt's house, and don't know she's gone yet." Curtis made a face at his brother. "I'll tell him to call you when he gets home."

"What did Mike want?" Walter stuttered as Curtis ended the call.

"Be cool and sit down. He's looking for Brenda." Curtis sighed, "A woman showed up at Mike and Pearl's tonight claiming to be Brenda's daughter."

"What! That's crazy. Brenda don't have no children." Walter threw up his hands and paced the floor. "Everything was going too well. We're doomed."

"Don't worry; several people will swear they saw your nutcase girlfriend leave. Just stick to the script." Walter walked over to his brother and put his arm around his shoulder. "You heard me tell Mike you weren't home when Brenda left."

"Since you told him I wasn't home, I don't need to call him."

"Why, so you can seem guilty of doing something?" Curtis walked over to the kitchen cabinet, removed a bottle of scotch, and two glasses. "Do you want a drink?"

"Yeah, I need one."

Curtis poured scotch into two glasses, handed one to Walter and took a sip out of the other. "Call Mike back and tell him you haven't seen Brenda. You were at your aunt's when she left. Did your girlfriend have a cell phone?"

"Yeah, it was in her purse. You probably threw it away when you packed her clothes."

Walter shook his head. "I hate talking to Mike."

"You hate it because you feel guilty about Linda and Asia."

"Wouldn't you?"

"Maybe I would, but all that's in the past. You can't change it, so stop letting it hold you captive."

"I guess you're right," Walter moaned.

"At some point, you gonna have to face leaving Asia, and try to make amends to her."

CHAPTER 8

Lieutenant Ray Hollis was the lead homicide detective six years ago when Eric died. Ray and his wife, Jay of four years, were at Mike and Pearl's house celebrating the grand opening of Eric's Place. They left the party after a young woman came and crashed it, claiming to be Brenda's daughter.

Therefore, Ray was not surprised when he received a call from Mike later that night. "Hey, thought I might hear from you after that scene at your house earlier."

"Can you believe it? This woman says she's my niece, and I didn't know she existed."

"Do you believe her?"

Mike sighed, "I don't know. She said Brenda was supposed to pick her up from the train station. She traveled here from Philadelphia."

"Have you been able to reach your sister?"

"Not yet." Mike paused, "Marie also told me Leroy Zackey is her father."

"Are you talking about the guy that was a big drug dealer about twenty years ago?"

"Yeah, he was a serious asshole back then." Mike added, "And I bet he still is."

"I've heard of Zackey, but his reign of terror was before I joined the department. I was a rookie in patrol when he went to prison." Ray sat back in his chair, "If this guy's on his way home, maybe Brenda's in hiding?"

"I don't think so. Marie showed me a picture of a house on which Brenda placed a deposit," Mike told Ray. "If she's afraid, why would she do that?"

"If this woman is telling the truth, you're right why'd Brenda put a deposit on a house if she's afraid of her husband?" Ray continued, "The other question is why didn't Brenda pickup her daughter from the train station?"

"It don't make sense," Mike concluded.

Ray paused, "Give me a couple of days to figure out what's going on and I'll get back to you as soon as I have something."

"Thanks man, I'll wait to hear from you," Mike responded as he ended the call.

Ray had a sinking feeling his gut. He had not felt this way since Eric's death, and recalled a homicide case a few years ago, that occurred in Philadelphia. He found the suspect hiding in Baltimore and made several contacts due to that

48

case. Ray figured he might need to ask one of them for help in getting information on Marie Zackey.

"Who was that?" Jay asked walking into the room as her husband ended the call.

"Mike."

"I'm not surprised, after what happened at his house tonight. Do you think the woman is Mike's niece?"

"Don't know, but I'll find out. Me and Mike became close friends during the investigation of Eric's death." Ray reached for his wife's hand, "Because of him I found the courage to approach you."

"Then, we both owe Mike," Jay smiled. "I'm going upstairs to bed. It's been a long day. Coming?"

"I'll be right up," Ray answered.

***

The lieutenant called his friend two days later in reference to Marie and Leroy Zackey. "Mike we should meet and talk? I think we need to include Asia, her husband, your wife, and Patty." Ray hesitated before adding, "Zackey was before Patty's time in the State's Attorney's Office, but there may still be someone that remembers him." He chuckled, "When my wife finds out, she'll want to come.

"We should meet tomorrow night at Eric's Place after the center closes," Mike suggested. "Asia will still be there and we can talk without worrying about Marie overhearing us."

"She's staying at your house?"

"Not happy about it, but my wife wouldn't let her go to a hotel."

"Be careful man, you don't know anything about her," Ray advised his friend.

"I'm as serious as a cancer patient with a heart attack, being careful around her." Mike hesitated before continuing, "I've got a terrible feeling about Marie and her father."

"I've collected information about Zackey and Marie, but haven't found any information that should cause you concern," Ray reported.

"I'm cool. Sometimes I worry too much." Mike sighed, "After what happened to Eric, I'm forever on alert."

"Understand, see you tomorrow."

***

Mike ended the call sitting at the kitchen table with his head in his hands. He had not seen Brenda in nineteen years since banning her from his home. Mike was angry when he told her and Walter to get out after realizing they were having an affair in his house while Asia's mother was dying. He shook his head thinking how it took him a long time to get over Eric's death and now

Marie appears. Mike wondered how Brenda could have kept a child, secret for so long.

Remembering that dreadful day his great nephew died, Mike still had regrets about not going to the barbershop with Asia and Eric. He wondered if his presence might have made a difference. There had been several incidents before Eric. Mike agonized over not realizing the danger he may have placed his family in by staying in the area.

It was a proud time when he purchased his house many years ago as an open door for love ones. Several members of his family lived in his house. Some stayed a few months while others remained for years. This home served as a lighthouse in their storms, and he wondered if another major front was on the way.

CHAPTER 9

"Where's Marie?" Ray asked entering Eric's
Place and finding the rest of the group present.
"Does she know we're meeting?"

"I told her it was a board meeting about the
center. Figured she might see us coming in here;
since she watches me and Pearl's every move."

"Good thinking Mike."

Pearl pointed her finger at her husband, "Cut
her some slack, she ain't got nobody."

The group entered Asia's office and took
seats around the desk. Ray walked over to the
window and watched the steady rain hit the
windowpane.

"I have information on Marie and her father."
Ray said as he left the window, picked up the
pad he had placed on Asia's desk, and looked

over his notes. "Let's start with Marie. I called in a favor and had a police friend in Philly leave call cards with several of the neighbors at the house where your niece lived with her aunt and uncle." Ray nodded at Mike and Pearl. "He also left several cards at the apartment building Marie and her aunt moved to after the uncle's death."

Ray sat on the corner of Asia's desk facing the group. "Only one person called back, and it was a strange conversation." He flipped through the pages of his yellow pad. "The caller was a young woman who lived in the house next door. She and Marie were friends. I wrote down her name, but don't see it." Ray again flipped the pages of his pad. "Anyway, she said the aunt was a small, quiet, sickly woman, and the uncle a nasty drunk."

"Yeah nice guys until they have a couple of drinks, then the devil comes out," Mike added.

"From what the neighbor said, you're right. She told me the aunt and Marie feared him." Ray returned to the window, talking as he watched the rain getting heavier.

"Did she tell you anything useful?" Patty asked twirling in her seat.

Ray turned from the window and faced Patty. "The neighbor talked about being awakened early in the morning by flashing lights and sirens of an ambulance. The uncle had a heart attack."

"What's strange about him having a heart attack?" Patty asked.

"The caller said when the paramedics went upstairs; they brought the uncle out of Marie's bedroom."

53

"Marie's bedroom?" Pearl placed her hand over her mouth.

"The neighbor said she asked Marie why the uncle was found dead in her bedroom."

"What did Marie say?" Pearl asked touching Ray's leg as he returned and sat at the end of Asia's desk.

"Marie told her friend they switched bedrooms that night so her aunt could be closer to the bathroom."

"Well, sounds logical," Pearl shrugged her shoulders.

"According to the neighbor it was strange as Marie's bedroom was small, and the uncle wasn't a man who would care about his wife being closer to the bathroom." Ray shifted on the edge of the desk. "She also said the difference in steps wouldn't have been significant."

"Oh." Pearl sat back in her chair.

"Most of the information on Zackey is ancient history, and Mike there may be things you know I didn't find."

"He was a low-life-drug dealer back in the late seventies, early eighties." Mike shook his head, "I can't believe Brenda would marry him or have a child by him. The girl called her Brenda Zackey."

"From the records I retrieved; Brenda was his wife and had his child."

"Good Lord," Pearl reached over and squeezed Mike's hand.

"From my research, Zackey was convicted in eighty-two and received twenty-five years for drug dealing. Ten years ago or more, the guy that testified against him was convicted of a

54

separate murder." Ray hesitated, "Somehow this witness was placed in the same facility with Zackey. I guess no one remembered, or it fell through the cracks."

"Did Big Zack get to him?" Mike moved to the edge of his seat.

"Not only did your sister's husband kill the former witness, but by the time the guards intervened, Zackey had eaten a piece of the guy's tongue."

No one said anything. The only sounds in the room were rain hitting against the windowpanes and the hollowing wind beating on the building.

"He was probably sending a message to the streets about anyone snitching on him." Mike stated breaking the silence. "You know these supposed-to-be-fake gangsters and their street reputations."

Ray shook his head, "It doesn't make sense as Zackey was close to coming home on parole. The doctors must have thought he was crazy as he was judged not criminally responsible for that murder." Ray shrugged his shoulders, "He's been at the Franklin Institution out there in Jessup since then. Where your nephew's been for the past few years," Ray said as he looked at Pearl.

"I wonder if they know each other," Mike asked turning to his wife.

"You can forget what you're thinking Mike. The answer is NO!" Pearl stood and continued, "Brian is not a low-life-thug psychopath like that guy."

Mike grunted, "That didn't stop Brian from trying to kill us to protect his life style."

"He was mentally sick and didn't know what he was doing," Pearl exclaimed.

"Your nephew is crazy as a fox. He may be evil, but that don't make him mentally ill."

"You don't understand what he went through when the so-called preacher murdered his mother."

"Aunt Pearl, we all got a story," Asia added. "It'd be helpful if someone could find out if Brian knows Zackey." Asia put her arms around her aunt. "Maybe we'd get information that might help find Aunt Brenda."

"I'm not asking my nephew to do anything that could put him in danger," Pearl stammered. "I know you and Mike haven't forgiven him, but its been six years. He's a different man now."

"Okay sweetie, we won't ask you to place your nephew in danger." Mike bent over and kissed Pearl's cheek. "We'll go home. It's getting late." Mike took Pearl's hand. "I'm taking my lovely wife home. Ray thanks for checking on Marie and her father."

Asia kissed her aunt on the cheek. "Sorry we upset you."

"It's fine," Pearl said through her sniffles as the rest of the group wished her and Mike good night.

Asia's husband wrapped his arms around his wife. "I should talk to Brian," he announced after Mike closed the door to the office. "If you all had not met him at my house in Boston, none of you would've ever been placed in danger."

"Believe me Winston; Brian was crazy before he met you," Patty shook her head. "The whole time he was pretending to be your friend. You didn't know his real name was Brian Adams. You thought it was Glenn Peck."

"I don't like that idea," Asia commented.

"There's someone who'd be perfect to talk to Brian," Jay spoke for the first time. "Tommie, remember they were childhood friends."

"Why in the world, would Tommie talk to Brian considering that lunatic tried to kill his sister, Shelia?" Asia erupted.

Jay frowned, "It doesn't hurt to ask him."

"No, we're not asking him!"

"Why? Asia, are you afraid you'll have to stop hating Tommie for not getting shot, instead of Eric?"

"Jay you're supposed to be my friend?"

"Yes, I am, and could've been killed with you the night that boy, Mad Dog, came to my house with a firebomb. Tommie didn't shoot Eric, or try to hurt us." Jay took Asia's hand. "Maybe it's time to bury your hatred with Mad Dog."

Asia pointed her finger at Jay, "But, it wasn't your child that died."

"No it wasn't but.... "

"That's enough Jay," Ray said as he held his wife, surprised at her behavior. Being seven-months pregnant must be affecting her. "Having Tommie talk to Brian may not be a good idea. Brian was responsible for Mad Dog being at your house, and he kidnapped Tommie's sister." Ray shook his head. "We'll think of something else."

"I agree with Jay about Tommie talking to Brian," Patty interrupted.

"Everybody's forgetting if not for Tommie, Eric would still be alive. Mad Dog was shooting at him, not my baby." Asia screamed with tears streaming down her face.

Patty took Asia's hand, "If it had been my son I would feel the same way, but it wouldn't bring him back." Patty waved her hand around, "Look at the great work you've done in your baby's name. You turned a place of sorrow into a safe haven and are giving hope to kids that need it."

Asia wiped the tears from her face, "Ray, it's a good idea. Jay's right childhood bonds are hard to break. It may not hurt to ask Tommie." She put her head on her husband's chest as he comforted her.

CHAPTER 10

Patty met her husband at the front door as she
arrived home from the center. Taking his wife's
raincoat John asked, "How was the meeting?
You look tired?"

"Much more difficult than I thought it would
be." Patty sat in the living room, took off her
shoes, and propped her feet on the ottoman.

"Would you like a glass of wine?"

"Yes, thanks I need it," Patty sighed.

"Why was the meeting so difficult?" John
poured a glass of wine for himself and Patty.
"Wasn't it about Mike's missing sister?"

"Yeah, that was the basic reason, but old
wounds were reopened." Patty took a sip of her
wine. "Remember the young woman that
showed up Saturday looking for Mike's sister,
claiming to be her daughter."

"Uh huh."

"Ray did a little research, and the girl is Brenda's daughter. The father's a drug dealer prominent in the late 70's and early 80's."

"The plot thickenings."

"Yeah, it gets better. The father's in Franklin Institution with Brian Adams."

"Brian Adams, Pearl's nephew?" John's brows rose.

"None other; and here's where the conversation got heated." Patty exhaled, "Jay suggested Tommie visit Brian to see if he knows the father, Leroy Zackey."

"Bet Asia wasn't happy with that idea."

"Not happy is an understatement. She and Jay got into it."

"Jay, that's surprising."

"Ray had to intervene."

"Wow, it got intense. I guess Pearl won't talk to him?"

"No, she left in tears at the mere mention of someone questioning Brian. She didn't want him put in danger."

"It's her nephew." John poured more wine into their glasses. "Is anybody going to talk to Brian?"

"After some back and forth, Asia agreed to the idea. The question is will Tommie do it after what Brian tried to do to his sister?"

"No wonder you look beat, sounds like it was emotional." John sat on the sofa, stroked Patty's shoulders, and kissed her sun-tint colored cheek.

"Okay Dr. Drake, what's your professional opinion of Tommie?"

"I helped him get a job in the hospital because of Sheila, but I've had limited interactions with him." John shrugged his shoulders. "He seems like a nice guy, and he works hard as far as I know."

Patty took a sip of her wine. "We can't get away from Brian Adams." She sighed, "The only real satisfaction I had was he spend most of the money he wanted to protect on lawyers and doctors so he could stay out of jail."

John chuckled, "I remember the day I came to court to observe, and he had more doctors testifying about his mental state than we had on staff."

"Don't get me wrong," Patty explained. "I'm sure he's got some serious issues, but he knew what he was doing was wrong and did it anyway." She took another sip of her wine. "Soon greed will be a defense."

"Maybe his issues are bigger than you think? He's been in Franklin for years."

"Yeah, but he should be doing ten to twenty in a prison, not a hospital. He tried to kill four people."

John poured the rest of the wine into their glasses. "Would you feel this way if they weren't your friends?"

Patty paused. "I don't know. Maybe my feelings wouldn't be as strong. What Brian did on top of losing Eric was devastating." She exhaled, "Asia didn't have time to grieve for her son before Brian made sure Mad Dog knew we were at Jay's house."

"I'm going upstairs," John said as he kissed her again.

61

"I'll be up shortly."

Patty leaned back on the sofa with her feet still on the ottoman and thought of the friendship she had with Asia. She recalled how she first met her friend about a year before Eric's death. Patty was interviewing a victim in her office when the woman became sick and vomited in a wastebasket. After the interview concluded, Patty carried the pail to the restroom. A woman with the most beautiful hazel eyes approached her.

"Excuse me Miss, where are you taking that container?" the hazel-eyed woman asked.

"Someone became sick in it, and I'm taking it to the restroom."

"No, that's my job, it's my first day." The woman smiled as she took the wastebasket from Patty's hand.

"Who are you?" Patty remembered asking.

"My name's Asia and you'll mess up your pretty clothes."

Patty reminisced how she and Asia became best friends, notwithstanding at the time, their social and economic dissimilarities. They had numerous things in common; both lost their mothers at young ages and had issues with their fathers. As the friendship between the women grew, the tough prosecutor began calling Asia's aunt and uncle, Aunt Pearl and Uncle Mike.

Patty sat drinking her wine recalling the hardships Asia had overcome. She was proud of her friend and grateful for the relationship they shared.

CHAPTER 11

Asia sat at her dressing table removing her makeup and preparing for bed. The meeting this evening with her friends and family had left her upset. Most of the time, Jay was soft-spoken, sweet, and always accommodating but not tonight.

Their disagreement over recruiting Tommie to help find her Aunt Brenda brought back memories. It took months before Asia could sleep through the night without waking to the screams of Mad Dog, rolling around Jay's yard on fire.

"I didn't plan to hurt the boy," she said as she removed Eric's framed photograph from her dressing table. "When I saw him approaching the house with the burning bottle, I reacted."

She ran her fingers around the frame as she spoke to her child's photograph.

Jay was right. She was angry with Tommie over her baby dying instead of him. *He chose that drug life.* "The bullet was meant for him not you," she said to her son's photograph as she placed the frame against her chest. Asia returned it to the table and took a deep breath.

She felt Ericka kicking in her stomach. "Calm down little girl. Mommy's okay." She rubbed her stomach and hummed a song her son sang from his favorite movie, *The Lion King.* "Your brother's in good hands. His grandmother has him."

She stared into the mirror, realizing what she said was true. Her mother had Eric, and he was safe in her love. "Eric's Place is about helping other children in my baby's name," Asia scolded her reflection. She reminded herself of a husband who without question loved her, two great stepchildren, family, and friends who had more than supported her through the most difficult times. In addition, she was grateful for the blessing on her way.

Asia retrieved her son's photo and recalled the game she played with Eric. They would spread their arms open and profess their love for one another. Six years had passed since then, but some days it felt like six minutes.

She replaced the photograph, lifted her shirt, and moved her hand over the spot on her side where Brian shot her. After he forced Sheila into the house and captured her family, he waved a gun around threatening them. Asia closed her eyes remembering how she charged him and the gun he was holding discharged. A bullet hit her in the side.

Consumed with anger; she ignored the pain and smashed his head against the oven he intended to use as a weapon. Brian had planned to disconnect the pipe and release gas into the room after he bound the four of them.

Tommie did not set out to hurt her or Eric, and maybe one day she could forgive him. Brian's actions were intentional and evil. She did not believe she would ever reach that goal with him.

Aunt Pearl maintained her nephew was mentally ill because of all the unfortunate events that happened to him as a child. Asia did not understand how her aunt could be so forgiving, but reminded herself that Aunt Pearl searched for Brian over thirty years. The young woman wondered how she would react if she had looked for a loved one that long. Asia stopped stroking her scar as her husband entered the room.

"Sweetheart, are you all right? It was a rough meeting tonight." Augustus retrieved the frame of her son from the dressing table. "You describe him as a happy little boy. I bet his brother and sister would had loved him.

"You mean sisters," Asia chuckled and pointed to her stomach. "She'll be here in three months."

Augustus smiled, "Remember the first time Lizzie saw you and said your skin was the color of her brown crayon."

Asia chuckled, "I laughed so hard, and you tried to die."

"It was the first time I heard you laugh, and it sounded like beautiful music. I believe I loved you even then." He lifted Asia to the bed and massaged her feet. "Are you sure you're okay?"

"I am now." She reared back on the bed, closed her eyes, and said a silent prayer of thanks.

CHAPTER 12

Leroy Zackey looked in the mirror as he freshened for his visit. Wednesday was the day Brenda came to see him, but the guard said it was a young woman named Marie Zackey. He was surprised and confused. He had not seen his daughter since she was a young girl with pigtails. Marie would be a woman now, and she may not even remember or recognize him.

Zackey recalled how prominent the Wallace genes were in his child. She had the deep skin coloring, hazel-colored eyes and sharp facial features of her maternal grandmother and uncle. Brenda and Linda were several shades lighter and didn't have hazel-colored eyes, but their features and bone structures were like the rest of the family.

The large man stared into the mirror and asked his bald-headed, earth-colored, full-faced image, if he was ready for this visit. A guard arrived to escort him to the dingy off-white cement room with block windows situated a few feet from the ceiling. The windows were large enough to let in sunlight, but too small for a body to enter or exit. A large glass window facing the hall kept the room from appearing as a large cell and provided data to the other inmates on who received visits.

Zackey watched his daughter walk through the metal detector as she entered the room and got directions to his table. Dressed in a black short sleeve shirt, long black ruffled skirt, and black canvas shoes; Zackey smiled thinking his daughter did not get her fashion style from her mother.

"Hello Leroy," she said as she sat across from him, and pushed her lips into a half smile.

I guess Dad would've been too much to expect. "Hi Marie, it's good to see you. Where's Brenda?"

"That's what I'm here to ask you. She was supposed to pick me up from the train station four days ago. She didn't show, and no one has seen her."

"What you mean no one has seen her?"

"Uncle Mike's been calling around, but nobody knows where she is."

"That's not like Brenda." Zackey answered realizing Mike is Uncle Mike and he's Leroy.

"I hope she's not playing a game because I quit my job and packed the apartment I had with your sister."

"You should know your mother better than that."

"I don't know her or you. The only person who looked out for me was Aunt Tissy, and she didn't always do a good job." Marie sucked her teeth and rolled her eyes.

The large man took a deep breath. "Marie, your mother and me made mistakes, but we took steps to insure you were taken care of." He nodded his head. "I gave money to Brenda before I went away and told her to make sure my sister got payments every month for your care."

"The problem with you and Brenda was you thought a few dollars every month made me well cared for." She leaned closer to her father, "But you'd be wrong, it didn't."

"What're you saying?"

"The only thing that money did was ease your conscience. Yeah, Brenda Clause came around two or three times a year when she went to New York to buy the junk she sells, bringing me ugly clothing and gaudy jewelry." Marie huffed, "But she didn't know what was going on with me." She pointed her finger at her father, "If you cared for me instead of getting revenge, or protecting your fucking street rep you could have saved me."

Zackey sat back in his chair and looked around the room to see if anyone heard his daughter. He was not accustomed to anyone talking to him this way. "It's obvious something awful happened to you. Please tell me?"

"Why, Leroy? You can't change it and I'm not the patient in this looney bin."

"Did you tell your mother what happened?"

"I blurted it out in anger after Aunt Tissy died, and Brenda pissed me off acting like she had been a good mother." Marie sat back waving her hand, "Might be why she asked me to come to Baltimore."

"Why did you come?"

"Brenda says she has twenty-thousand dollars and I need that money. You both owe me."

"Have you told your mother how you feel?"

"No, she lives on another planet and believes the three of us will live together like in some silly ass fairy tale, but I will as soon as I find her."

Zackey looked in his daughter's eyes; he could swear they now looked black instead of hazel. "I'm sorry I wasn't there for you, but I'm coming home soon and I can try to make it up to you." The large man extended his arm, reached across the table, and put his hand on top of his daughter's hand. "You only hurt yourself when you carry hatred in your heart."

"Did you learn that in a therapy session?" Marie answered pulling away.

"Yeah, I did. Please tell me what happened. Put that burden on me." Zackey again extended his hand. "Like you said, I owe you."

Marie folded her arms. "Maybe one day, but right now I need to find Brenda. Do you know where she is or someone who might?"

Zackey sat back in his seat, closed his eyes, and exhaled. "Your mother's been living with a man named Walter Jones for the past nineteen years."

"Who is he? How'd you get this information, and why was she living with him?" She leaned

closer to her father. "Do you have a phone number or an address for him?"

"I don't have either. Brenda used a post office box when she communicated with me and later we talked on her cell phone." Marie's father hung his head, "But your Uncle Mike may have a way to reach Walter."

"Uncle Mike, how?"

"Walter is Asia's father."

"What!"

"Please lower your voice, Marie."

"How could Brenda been with Asia's father all these years? She must've slept with him right after her sister died, or was it before?"

"Don't judge your mother, she made mistakes."

"For nineteen years?"

"You don't understand. It might sound bad, but she was alone and vulnerable."

"Brenda ain't ever been vulnerable in her life. If you were so concerned why you kill that guy in prison?"

"You're right and if you want to blame someone, let it be me."

"I blame you and her. You two are more disgusting than I could ever imagine," Marie stood, rolled her eyes at her father, and left.

CHAPTER 13

The young woman shielded her eyes from the
sun as she exited the visiting room building.
Marie saw a candy wrapper paper on the ground
and kicked it as she scurried back to the charter
bus she caught to come visit her father.

She was the first one to return to the bus.
Marie entered and walked to the rear. Hoping
not to invite any meaningless small talk with the
driver or returning passengers.

This visit proved to her that Leroy and
Brenda were both crazy and belonged together
in their three-ring circus. "I bet Walter's too
stupid to realize he's part of a circus." She said
aloud and looked to the front of the bus to insure
the driver did not hear her. Marie was relieved

when she noticed the driver smoking a cigarette outside the bus and sighed as she vowed to find her mother.

She was angry with her father, but furious with Brenda, who never said she was sleeping with Asia's father. Marie was not sure what her next move should be, or even what to believe. If Brenda withheld information about sleeping with Asia's father for nineteen years, maybe she lied about having the money. *I hope Brenda's not lying.*

Leroy was the real surprise. With everything, her aunt told her, he did not seem like someone who would go along with his wife living with another man and still deal with her. Marie figured being locked-up left her father little choice, and Brenda was staying with Walter and saving money until her husband came home. The young woman wondered if her mother's actions were romantic or just plain devious.

Mulling thoughts around in her head, Marie decided to ask Aunt Pearl and Uncle Mike to help her file a missing person's report on her mother. They would have to give the police Walter's address, and she would listen and commit it to memory.

Marie was so deep in thought; she did not realize the other passengers were aboard until the bus was full. She sat back and closed her eyes during the return ride to Baltimore, confident of her plan.

Returning home, Marie found Mike and Pearl sitting at the kitchen table. Pearl looked as if she had been crying—*must have been some board meeting*. Marie considered waiting until the morning to bring up the subject, but could visualize Aunt Tissy scolding her about not doing things right away.

"Uncle Mike and Aunt Pearl, it's been four days and we haven't heard anything from my mother," Marie said in the most concerned voice she could muster. "Do you think we should file a missing person's report? Something might have happened to her."

"You're right Marie. This is strange even for Brenda. I can't see her telling you to come here and leaving you stranded at the train station." Mike turned to his niece, "You sure you were supposed to come last Saturday?"

"Uncle Mike, my mother purchased the train ticket."

"Should we call and tell the police to come here or go to Curtis and Nicky's house?" Pearl asked.

"We should send them to Curtis' house since she was last living there. I have the address in my book." Mike went into the living room and pulled out his book from a table holding several loose papers. "I know the street and house but can't remember the number. Here it is Pearl, 10119 W. Lanvale Street."

"Is that far from here Uncle Mike?"

"No, if you go to the end of the block and cut through the park, it's the next block. Why, you going there?" he laughed.

"No, just trying to learn Baltimore," Marie grinned.

Pearl tapped Mike's arm, "We should do it tomorrow. It's kinda late to send the police to Curtis and Nicky's house."

"Yeah, you're right, sweetie. We'll wait till tomorrow to call the police. What's one more day?"

Mike placed his head in his hand, "Every time I contact Curtis it's about bad news."

"It's time for you and Curtis to makeup."

Mike exhaled, "Maybe."

"You've been angry with Curtis all these years over something he didn't do," Pearl informed.

"He didn't denounce it."

"It was his brother. Um... we should talk it over later," Pearl, said nodding toward her niece.

"Don't worry Aunt Pearl; I know about Brenda and Asia's father."

"What, how did you find out? I can't believe Brenda told you."

"No she didn't. It's a long story." Marie answered not caring one way or another as she had the information she needed.

CHAPTER 14

Brian realized the visit did not go well when he observed the expression on his roommate's face. Wednesday visits with Brenda left the big man in a good mood, but today Zackey looked as if a herd of elephants had trampled him.

"I take it, the visit didn't go well," Brian said working on his crossword puzzle.

"No lie."

"Want to talk about it?"

"Not now, thanks."

"If you change your mind I'm here, not going anywhere."

"True," Zackey nodded his head and sat on the bed with his eyes closed.

"Just remember, you're on your way out. Don't let nothing or nobody stop you."

Brian knew his roommate would talk when he was ready. They had a good relationship now, but it did not start that way.

"Hey Zack, remember the big fight we had when we first became roommates?"

"Nope, I don't."

"Yeah, you do. Next, you'll say you don't remember calling me White Girl."

"Awe, I was just kidding?"

"Kidding my ass: you meant it."

"I did until you banged me in my mouth. Man, you ain't slick, trying to get my mind off my daughter." Zackey laughed, "I know how you operate."

"Is it working?"

The big man exhaled, "I'm cool. It is—what it is."

Brian smiled as he remembered the scene between the two of them when he arrived at Franklin and landed in a room with his tormentor. Later, Brian discovered he was the third person to have the honor of sharing Zackey's room.

The bully called Brian names and often bumped the smaller man when walking pass on purpose. Brian was terrified but afraid to ask the staff to move him. He believed it was best not to show fear as it could give other patients an excuse to torment him.

The intimidation went on for months. One Sunday, while Aunt Pearl was visiting, Brian observed his roommate walk pass the large glass window in the visiting room.

"Hey White Girl," Zackey shouted when Brian returned to their room. "You were with this middle-age black woman in the visiting room. What you got, grandma jungle fever?"

"That's my Aunt Pearl," Brian screamed as he charged his roommate, noticing the surprised expression on Zackey's face. The rage Brian felt was overwhelming as he thought back to the abuse he received as a child because of his light complexion and gray-colored eyes. His anger intensified by the guilt he felt for trying to murder the one person who loved him: Aunt Pearl.

Brian continued hitting his roommate with all his strength, avoiding the swings of his opponent by moving and ducking. He tried not to let the larger man hit him. However, after a few seconds Zackey landed a blow and knocked Brian to the floor.

"Stop before I kill your little punk ass, White Girl, and I'm faced with another murder charge," the large man yelled.

"My name is not White Girl," Brian screamed with blood pouring from his mouth.

"What the hell is going on in here?" The hospital security officer asked upon entering the room.

"I fell," Brian replied.

"What you do, fall off a mountain?"

"I said I fell."

"What's with you, Zackey?" The officer inquired, "You fall too?"

"Nah, he fell on me. I should sue this damn place."

The guard pointed his finger and threatened, "You ain't suing nobody. You two must think I'm stupid. This better be the end of it since you two wanna play games."

Brian stopped reflecting on the past and looked at his friend still sitting on the bed with his eyes closed. Whatever happened between Zackey and his daughter had to be serious. He had been roommates with this man for many years, and this was the first time he saw his friend rattled. Brian wondered where the daughter had been, and why Brenda, did not come with her.

During Zackey's visit with his daughter, Brian walked past the visiting room. His roommate's daughter was not what he expected. She was dressed in all black, not like her mother who wore colorful flamboyant outfits. The young woman appeared familiar. Brian was sure he had never met her and knew his roommate would not give out any information until he was ready.

CHAPTER 15

Jay parked in front of Thelma's house, which was between her old house and Sheila's. The former neighbor remembered the good times the women had together. They were like the three Musketeers and always looked out for each other.

Smiling, Jay recalled how six years ago Thelma was angry when she asked her to help paint the banister and front door. It was to prepare for what was supposed to be Asia's going away celebration. Jay cringed remembering how Mad Dog showed up the night of the party with a firebomb. She was glad there was no burn marks left on the front yard from the fire that claimed his life.

"Little boy you got me fat and emotional," Jay said to her unborn child patting her stomach as she felt him kicking. She sat in the car preparing to talk to Thelma and Sheila. Jay was not sure how Sheila would react, but knew her best friend Thelma could be tough.

Watching, Tommie and Thelma's son, Marcus, playing catch across the street in the park she laughed. *Good thing Marcus is an intellectual cause he is no athlete.* She sat collecting her nerves as Marcus missed more balls than he caught.

Jay checked her lipstick in the car mirror and smoothed her long brown hair back from her cinnamon-colored face. She took a deep breath, unhooked her seat belt, and slid her long shapely legs from under the steering wheel.

"Girl, you look as if you're about to explode," Thelma said, as she reached out to help Jay up the stairs of the front porch. "Were you this big with your daughter?"

"No, and I was younger. I'm too old for this."

"You're beautiful and look so cute pregnant." Shelia walked out of Thelma's house and patted Jay's stomach.

"Oh please," Thelma rolled her eyes.

"Woo." Jay exclaimed. "I need to sit and glad you have real porch furniture, not the beat-up chair you found in the alley."

"Don't give her any credit. Tommie bought this furniture."

"I was getting to it."

Sheila rolled her eyes. "When Thelma? You had that broken chair on the porch for years."

"It wasn't on the priority list."

"I feel you," Jay reclined and propped her feet.

81

"How long do you plan on working?" Thelma asked shaking her head.

"As long as I can, Patty was busy as an Assistant Attorney, but now she's the State's Attorney, and crazy busy."

"She needs to hire another person, can't put everything on you." Thelma looked at Sheila as she threw up her hands.

"Patty will when she can. This is the city; we don't have the budget that most of the counties have," Jay explained.

"What'd Ray say?" Thelma asked.

"He said to use my judgment."

"Smart man," Thelma smiled, exposing her gold tooth as she smacked Shelia's hand. "Want some ice tea?"

Sheila warned, "It's got a ton of sugar in it."

"Everybody ain't trying to be a health nut," Thelma replied as she stroked her tight, size fourteen jeans.

Jay smiled, "Sure, I'm pregnant that's my excuse to eat and drink whatever I want."

"Where's your daughter?" Thelma asked as she gave her friend a glass of the sweet tea.

Taking a sip Jay answered, "My husband took the kids to the movies."

"Good thing, my child can't catch the ball now. If your daughter was here, he'd be a real wreck."

"Marcus had it bad for your daughter since they were toddlers," Shelia laughed.

"He don't care nothing about playing catch. Something's on his mind he wants to talk to Tommie about," Thelma told Jay as Marcus missed another ball.

"What could it be?" Jay asked concerned.

"Not sure, but I can tell he's been bothered about something. I bet it's got to do with that school, Asia's husband helped get him in."

"Thelma it's a good school and a great chance for him."

"Jay, it's just Marcus don't fit into those private school kids' life."

"Let him work it out. He gonna meet all kinds of people in this world," Jay insisted. "He's not alone; Win is his classmate and friend, isn't he?"

"Yeah, and he got my brother to keep him balanced, and make sure he has some street smarts," Shelia added.

"I don't know," Thelma moaned, as she sat in the chair opposite her friend. "So, what's up Jay? What brings you out into this heat to the poorer side of town?"

"Funny, Thelma. Remember I lived next door, but I'd like to talk to both of you."

"What is it?" Thelma asked as she looked at Sheila.

"I need... we need Tommie to do us a big favor."

"Who is we and why are you talking to me and Thelma instead of my brother?"

"Because if either of you have objections, I won't ask Tommie."

"So who is we?" Thelma repeated.

"Me, Ray, Patty, Winston, and Asia...."

"Asia," Thelma and Sheila shrieked in unison.

"She don't want nothing to do with my brother," Shelia exclaimed.

83

Thelma rolled her eyes, "If Asia wants anything from my man, she should come off her high horse and ask him herself."

"It was my idea. Asia went along with it."

Jay took a deep breath. "Remember last Saturday when a woman interrupted the party claiming to be Mr. Mike's niece?"

"Yeah, that was wild," Sheila, replied and exchanged expressions with Thelma.

"This concerns her." Jay gave her friends the information about the niece. "Mr. Mike's sister is missing and the woman's father is in Franklin with Brian." Jay hesitated, "I was hoping Tommie could talk to his childhood friend and see if Brian knows the father, Leroy Zackey." Jay shifted her position in the chair. "If he does, maybe Brian can get information that might help find Mr. Mike's sister."

"You want my brother to go to the psyche ward and talk to that lunatic?" Sheila's small-framed body shook.

"Jay, you couldn't come up with a better idea than this? What about Ms. Pearl?" Thelma persisted, "It's her nephew, let her ask him." Thelma put her arms around Sheila.

"She won't," Jay, answered dropping her eyes.

"And neither will my brother," Sheila replied as tears fell from her large eyes. "Have you forgotten how he planned to kill me, Asia, and her family?"

"No, I haven't. I'm sorry Sheila; didn't mean to upset you. I know what you went through with Brian." Jay sighed and hung her head, "Just thought with Tommie and Brian being childhood friends...."

"What about me and Brian?"

The three women stopped talking. Tommie stood on the porch with Marcus behind him.

"We didn't hear or see you guys come up the stairs," Thelma responded and told Marcus to go into the house.

"What about me and Brian?" Tommie repeated, "And why are you crying, Sheila?"

"It's my fault, and it may be time for me to leave," Jay pushed up from the recliner.

"Is anyone gonna answer my question?" Tommie demanded.

"Go ahead, tell him," Thelma wrapped her arms around Tommie's waist.

Jay repeated the information she had given to her two friends. No one said anything until she finished.

Tommie leaned against the porch wall and closed his eyes. The three women were silent as he stood there. "I'll do it," he said after a few seconds.

"Sweetheart, you sure that's a good idea?" Thelma took his hand, "How will you react to seeing him?"

"Every nerve in my body will want to smash in his face, but I won't."

"You don't have to do this," Thelma stammered.

"I'm not trying to get Asia's approval, but I regret what happened to her son," Tommie sighed.

Thelma placed her head on Tommie's chest. "You didn't shoot her child."

"No, I didn't but Mad Dog was shooting at me."

Jay stood and placed her hand on Tommie's arm, "You aren't responsible for what happened to Eric. Maybe going to see Brian is not such a good idea."

"Don't worry I won't hurt him because I've got too much to lose." Tommie lifted Thelma's hand to his lips and kissed it. "I'm not doing this out of any guilt, but because Asia and her family been through hell—whether or not it's my fault. If I can help, I will."

CHAPTER 16

Sheila went into her bathroom and took two aspirins out of the medicine cabinet for her aching head. She was glad Tommie was still next door at Thelma's house. It gave her time to get herself together.

Jay's mention of Brian upset her. Sheila previously knew him as Glenn Peck before discovering he was the one behind Mad Dog being at Jay's house with a fire cocktail on the night of Asia's celebration.

The next day Brian disguised as a delivery person showed up at her house with a large, beautiful plant. Once she opened the door, he shoved her and pushed his way inside her home. Entering, he pulled out a gun, "Don't scream, or try to run," he warned.

Her slender body shook as she remembered how frightened she was looking at a gun pointed at her. She sobbed as tears fell from her large attractive eyes. "I don't have much money, but you can take what I've got. Please don't hurt me," she pleaded with her lips trembling.

"I won't hurt you," he said. "But I need you to cooperate with me by taking me to Asia's house."

She recognized the voice of the intruder from their many phone conversations. It sounded like her brother's friend, Glenn Peck. "How do you know Asia? I'm not taking you to her house," she insisted shaking her head.

"Don't you realize I have a gun?" The disguised driver said as he forced Sheila to his delivery van. "I'll shoot you if you make me." He opened the door and shoved her into the front passenger seat. "Stop crying," he grumbled. "Fasten your seat belt and don't try anything stupid. I can shoot faster than you can run."

Sheila tried not to reflect on that day. It was painful. She wiped her eyes and retrieved two letters hidden in her dresser drawer Brian had written to her. The letters begged for forgiveness and offered to help her return to school to earn a registered nurse's license. She shook her head realizing how much information she shared with Brian (Glenn Peck) Adams during their talks. Including, but not limited to information on her mother, wanting to be a registered nurse, and regrets of not being married or having children.

She thought he was only trying to help her brother. "*I was stupid.*" Shelia hid the two letters under the covers on her bed as Tommie entered the room.

"You okay, little sis?" Tommie sat on Sheila's bed and held her hand.

"Yeah, I'm good, but you shouldn't go to see Brian."

"I ain't happy about the idea, after what he did to you."

She wiped her nose, "Don't worry about me. I didn't expect you home so early?"

"I left to give Marcus and Thelma a chance to talk." He leaned back on the bed. "Marcus is a bright kid, but he don't know how to take-up for himself."

"Are the kids at school giving him a hard time?"

"Yeah," Tommie groaned. "Kids can be cruel, especially when there's someone of a different race who appears weak."

"Have they got physical with him?"

"Not yet, just calling him names."

"What names?" Sheila stood and balled her fist.

"All right Angela Davis," Tommie laughed. "You look as if you're ready to kick ass."

"I love Marcus, and Thelma's not the most diplomatic person." Sheila groaned, "She'll go up to that school and turn it out."

"Yes, Thelma can be a little rough around the edges, but loves her son and won't embarrass him." Tommie shook his head. "Marcus gonna have to learn how to handle difficult people."

"It makes me angry when people try to hurt someone I love," Sheila moaned.

"I've a good friend that teaches karate at a rec center on the west side."

Sheila looked puzzled, "Who's this friend? I've never heard you talk about him."

"I met him in jail."

"Where you say?" she shrieked.

"Sheila, every person in jail, is not bad. Besides, he's a prison guard."

"You're right. I shouldn't judge."

Tommie added, "It'll teach Marcus discipline and how to protect himself, along with boosting his self-confidence."

"You seem to care for Thelma and Marcus? How serious are you two?"

"Been waiting to see how long it would take you to ask me that question." Tommie laughed, "We're taking it slow. I've got work to do before I can commit to another person." He paused, "I've got to do this right. If not, Marcus and Thelma could be hurt."

"You care for them, so what's the problem?"

"I'm late on some things."

"Like what?"

"I appreciate the job you and Dr. Drake got me. Trust me, I'll be like the mailman every day on that bus corner going to work through heat, cold, and snow."

"You crazy," Sheila laughed.

"But no matter how hard I work, I'm never gonna be able to give Thelma a big house like her friend Asia has."

Shelia shook her head, "Trust me, Thelma don't care nothing about big houses or fancy cars."

"Maybe, but before we go down this road, we must be sure." Tommie pushed himself up from the bed and felt paper rattling under the covers.

"What's this?" he asked removing two letters from under the thin top spread.

"It's not what you think."

"These letters are from Brian. How long have you had them?"

Sheila hung her head, "A few months."

Tommie stood with the letters in his hand. "You still have them? Why are you holding on to them?"

"I don't know."

"Please tell me you don't have feelings for that maniac?"

"No—I hate him."

"Sheila, you don't keep letters from a person you hate!" Tommie sat up on the bed and put his head into his hands. "My fault, wish I hadn't asked you to contact Brian about getting me a lawyer." Tommie sighed, "I was afraid when they arrested me, and wasn't thinking straight."

"You had no idea what he'd do," she moaned.

"Yeah, but I talked to him several months before the shooting. I should've seen Brian was unstable. He was even using a fake name."

"You're not a doctor, he fooled people."

"Then explain it to me baby-sis."

"I wish I could. "You think I'm stupid—don't you?"

"No, I don't." Tommie put his arms around his sister. "You missed a lot during the years you took care of Momma." He took Sheila's small hands into his. "They were your teenage years. You should've been carefree, and I'm sorry for that."

"Don't feel guilty. I wouldn't change those times for anything in the world." She held her brother's hand. "I loved Momma, and she loved me, just as I love you. If I had to do it again, I would. It was a big sacrifice for both of us." She hugged him, "Me and Momma could not have survived without the money you sent us, and I understand why you sold..."

Tommie interrupted, "No excuses, and it's in the past, but Brian tried to kill you to protect his money and position."

"I know," she sighed.

"So please help me understand why you kept the letters?"

"Maybe because I need to heal, and not fall apart when I hear Brian's name," she answered with her voice crackling. "It seems like I'm stuck in my pain. Everyone else has moved on, even Asia."

Tommie kissed his sister on the cheek, "Don't compare your pain to anyone else's. It could be time you talked to a therapist." He chuckled, "We work in a hospital, it's time we used our connections."

"You're right," Sheila smiled.

"Just remember I'm here for you," Tommie said embracing his sister.

CHAPTER 17

Brian watched his childhood friend clear the metal detector and head to his table. It been several years since he had seen Tommie, and his friend was different. The gaudy jewelry, baggy sweat suit, and sneakers were gone. Tommie had lost weight and appeared more muscular than Brian remembered. The deep yellow polo shirt Tommie wore with black trousers highlighted his dark complexion. Brian realized that Tommie no longer like a drug dealer.

Amused, Brian smiled as he observed several women in the room noticing his friend. What made it even more humorous was Tommie did not apprehend the charisma he possessed as he charged toward Brian like a man on a mission.

"How are you, Tommie? Glad to see you."

"Let's get this straight; this ain't no social visit," Tommie answered as he sat across from Brian.

"I figured as much, hear you've been home a while."

"Listen to me," Tommie lowered his voice as he leaned closer to Brian. "The only thing that keeps me from pulling your head off your body is I got too much to lose."

"Why're you here?" Brian scooted back in his seat.

"Man, I protected you and to thank me, you try to kill my sister. For what—material shit?"

"If you came here to tell me what a terrible person I am, you've wasted you're time. I already know." Brian looked Tommie in the eyes and pleaded, "I'd change a lot of things if I could, but can't and I'm very sorry."

"Whatever," Tommie growled. "I'm here for a different reason. This woman showed up last Saturday claiming she was Mr. Mike's niece." Tommie sat back in his seat. "She's looking for her mother, who is missing. The woman's father is in here with you, Leroy Zackey. Do you know him?"

"Suppose I do, what's it got to do with the missing mother?"

"Because genius, he may know where she is?"

"Calm down Tommie, just asking. Why didn't my aunt ask me?"

"As usual, she's trying to protect your sorry ass. She said Zackey is a lunatic, and she didn't want you put in danger by asking questions."

Brian laughed, "She's right he is, but then so am I."

"Do you have any information that may help find the mother?" Tommie grumbled.

Taking a deep breath, Brian sat back in his chair and closed his eyes. He recalled the times his friend protected him from the cruelty of the neighborhood children.

He replayed how Tommie came to his rescue after they had not seen each other in thirty years. It was the night Brian's wife died, and he went out walking to clear his head. A scary-looking man approached him and pointing a knife at his throat. Brian remembered the fear he felt when the knife-yielding man ordered, "Give me your wallet. Don't think I won't stab you." He was even more afraid when the man repeated his command.

There was a loud screech of wheels from a nearby car, and a large, dark figure climbed out of the driver's side and advanced to the armed man holding a knife to Brian's neck.

Tommie asked the man, "Didn't anyone ever tell you not to bring a knife to a gun fight," and placed a silver object to the back of the knife-yielding-man's head. "Get out of here before I shoot your sorry ass."

"Mike's niece was here a few days ago, and Zackey was upset when she left." Brian said as he opened his eyes. "I don't think he knows where the mother is." Brian paused, "I've been the man's roommate the whole time I've been here, and I've never seen him so upset."

"Thanks, if you hear something helpful, call me. I'll leave my number at the desk." Tommie paused before adding, "Don't contact my sister anymore."

"Shouldn't Sheila make that decision?"

"I'm telling you don't contact my sister again. Do you understand?" Tommie barked.

"I can't excuse what I did, but that was six years ago." Brian hung his head, "I wish you could forgive me... I wrote to Sheila because I've changed."

"I don't believe you. I may not be a doctor or have a degree, but I know people. You acted out of pure greed, lied, and were willing to steal and kill to possess your wife's money and power." Tommie pointed his finger at Brian. "You're nothing more than a slimy little snake, just because you're not hissing doesn't make you any less of a dangerous snake."

"Man, we were once friends, and you of all people know what I went through as a child."

"Yeah and once is right." Tommie smacked the table, "You aren't the only one to face hard times." He grunted, "You had a chance after your father and his wife died to make a life that didn't include killing people." Tommie frowned and shook his head at his former friend. "Man you can go anywhere and be treated with dignity, because of how you look."

"So you're like everyone else, judging me on my appearance."

"Don't try to lay that guilt trip on me. Save it for somebody who cares like your aunt, hear me don't contact my sister again."

"You don't need to protect Sheila from me. I won't try to hurt her."

"Damn right you won't," Tommie stood ready to leave. "You don't know the emotional harm you inflicted on my sister."

"I'm sorry, and maybe one day I can earn her forgiveness and yours."

"That day will never come."

Returning to his room after the visit, Brian sat on his bed with his knees pulled up to his chest. He wondered if his former friend was right about him being a snake, considering how his wife died.

Brian recalled being in Baltimore with his wife at an affair for her father at the Arch Hotel. During the event, they returned to the room because she complained of being tired. As soon as they entered their room, sweat moistened her face. His wife was twenty years older with a heart condition. She clutched her chest and removed a nitroglycerin pill from her handbag. Brian hit her hand with such force the pill flew in the air and landed on the other side of the room. He could still remember the shocked expression on his wife's face as she fell to the floor. Brian stood over his wife as she took her last breath. He had no remorse for her death, only joy at inheriting her estate.

Zackey entered the room and saw Brian sitting on the bed rocking with his head on his knees.

"Looks like you're the one with the bad visit this time."

"Yeah, it was an old friend."

"A friend made you look like that?"

"We're not friends anymore."

"No kidding," Zackey laughed. "Why?"

Brian looked down at the bed and let out a loud sigh. "It's a very long story. Let's say he has every right to feel the way he does."

"Look man your past can't be any worse than mine. I've done horrible things. What's up with your friend?"

"His name is Tommie, and we were friends. We grew up in this little dark hole called Yellow Pond in South Carolina," Brian explained in a strained voice as he walked to the window and stared through the bars. "Tommie protected me as a child from the neighborhood bullies who taunted me because of my appearance. You know what I mean don't you?"

Zackey exhaled, "I'm sorry about the way I treated you when you first came here."

Chuckling Brian stated, "That's behind us now. Anyway, my aunt moved to Baltimore and sent for me, and my mother. We were so happy, but before we could leave, Momma went up the street to get her pay for cleaning the church."

Brian stood staring out the window for a few moments before continuing. His voice cracked, "I waited for her, but my mother never came back. The preacher and his wife came and forced me into their car. We drove for hours before they stopped."

Zackey sat on the corner of his bed. "What happened to your mother?"

"I found out later the preacher killed her by pushing her down the church steps."

"Why did he take you?"

"Maybe guilt... one night when he was drunk, he told me I was his son, but it didn't make sense. His wife terrorized me, and he let her."

"How long did this go on?"

"From the time I was seven until I was almost eighteen."

"Did you leave when you turned eighteen?

"Not until they died in a fire. Then I left."

Zackey frowned, "Okay, what happened after they died."

"I continued to use the name the preacher gave me, Glenn Peck, and roamed around for a few years. Met and married an older woman who had money, power, and position." Brian turned from the window and faced his roommate. "It was the first time I ever had anything, and it felt good." Brian returned to the window observing the lawn maintenance workers cutting the grass. "After she died, nothing and no one was more important than holding on to that money and power. I had told so many lies; I was afraid her family would come after my money."

Brian sat on the edge of his bed and faced his roomate, "Tommie hates me because I tried to kill his sister, my aunt, uncle, and cousin so no one could expose me. I didn't want to jeopardize losing my fortune."

Zackey cleared his voice, "Not sure what to say. I've never tried to hurt a love one."

"Believe me; I didn't love anyone at the time. Not even myself."

"Hey man like you told me; don't let your past hold you hostage."

"Good advice, but I'm not sure I will ever escape my past... ever."

CHAPTER 18

"Lila, I've been here a week and no closer to finding Brenda or the money," Marie said on her Nokia cell phone to her friend.

"Where are you now?" Lila asked.

"I'm sitting in this poor excuse of a park, trying to keep an eye on the boyfriend's house." Marie shook her head. "Seen an older couple come and go, but not anyone who might be this Walter guy," she explained looking at the house.

"Did the police go to the boyfriend's and ask about your mother?

Marie kicked a pebble in front of the bench as she continued talking, "Yeah, the police went there, talked to the neighbors, and everyone swears they saw Brenda get in her car and leave Saturday night."

"If you don't find Brenda, I may have to ask my neighbor to help me save my grandmother's house."

"Please... don't accept any money from that creep, Rudolph Rudy," Marie screamed. "I hate him. I promise I'll get the money," Marie stumbled. "Wait a minute—call you back, a guy just left the house heading this way."

Marie was shaking as she ended her phone call. She had to find her mother and get the money before Lila got it from her neighbor. A medium-built man around five feet ten, and dark wavy hair with gray streaks carrying a thin briefcase walked by her. He looked at the ground, and not at her. The man sat on a bench several feet away with his head in his hands. Marie watched him rocking and talking to himself. She tried to be discreet, but realized he was oblivious to her presence.

This had to be Walter, she reasoned. His odd behavior struck her as a man Brenda could control. He continued to look at the ground, talked to himself, and wrung his hands. The man kept looking in his brief case as if the contents would disappear.

She became bored and annoyed with him and glanced around at her surroundings. The park had seen better days. The children's swings did not have seats at the end of the chains. She discovered earlier that the large water faucet in the center of the park was not working. Many of the benches were broken, and others needed painting.

It was early Saturday morning, but only a few people were in the park. One or two individuals walked their dogs, and there was a group of old men sitting several seats in the opposite direction. She heard them arguing and debating over nothing much she figured.

Marie looked back at the man she believed was Walter and realized he was leaving the bench. He proceeded to the park entrance and down the street. She followed him as he passed Uncle Mike and Aunt Pearl's house, crossed the street, and entered Eric's Place.

She was surprised. From her talks with Aunt Pearl, Marie did not think Asia and her father were close. She wanted to follow him into the center but could not think of an excuse. Instead, she took advantage of the nice day, and sat on her uncle's front steps to wait and see what would happen next. The cell phone rang, but Marie did not answer it since she had no more information to report.

Lila's home was in Dewey, Delaware, fifteen minutes from Rehoboth Beach. The beach town was appealing to the two women. So far, they paid fifteen-thousand from the insurance monies they combined. After funeral costs, Lila had four-thousand from her great aunt and six from her grandmother. Marie had five from Aunt Tissy's insurance policy.

"It's a shame my aunt, your grandmother, and great aunt paid on these policies for years to wind up with such small amounts of money," Marie told Lila as she gave her the money from her aunt's policy. To take care of the balance, the women needed the money Brenda claimed to have.

Marie leaned back against the cool marble steps with the sun beating on her face. I have to get this money, she thought as she closed her eyes and fantasized about her friend and lover. Touching her breasts with light strokes and caressing her thighs, she envisioned Lila's beautiful bronze face with her large almond shaped eyes. Despite the lack of love in her life, the feelings she had for Lila were real.

The two women met when they were both fifteen, and it had been a bad year for them. Lila lost her parents in a murder-suicide. Marie told Lila part of her secret, but not the entire story. Sharing, everything was something Marie could not bring herself to do.

Lila lived with her maternal grandmother, Ellie in Dewey during the school year and her great aunt in Philadelphia next door to Marie and Aunt Tissy during the summer. For years, they were two teenagers trying to reach normal. Marie and Lila helped each other heal and fell in love.

Marie remembered the first time she mentioned to her friend about living in Philly during the summer. "It should be the other way around," she teased. "Who wants to live in a beach town in the winter and Philly in the summer?"

Lila laughed, "I spend the beginning and end of summer in Delaware. That's the best time, fewer people." The young woman smiled and looked at Marie. "Plus, I'm with you most of the summer. Can't beat that?"

Marie smiled. "Always looking for the positive, I'll be like that someday."

Engrossed into her fantasy, Marie heard her name called, and jumped. Aunt Pearl was at the front door asking if she wanted breakfast.

"Yeah, Aunt Pearl, I'm hungry," she answered not knowing when Walter might leave the center. She wondered how long Aunt Pearl had been at the door.

"It'll just be the two of us. Mike is over at Eric's Place."

"That's nice."

"The center's been opened less than a week, but Mike is having a ball working with the kids."

"From the short time I've known him, I'm not surprised," Marie responded following her aunt into the house.

"You had a nightmare last night," Pearl said as she placed a platter of bacon and bowls of eggs and biscuits on the table. "Are you okay?"

"I hope I didn't wake you guys?"

"Don't matter, what's important is you. Marie, you can tell me anything." Pearl walked around the table and put her arms around her niece. "We didn't know about you, honey. If we had, we would've been in your life."

"Don't worry, I'm okay."

Pearl returned to her seat. "You're not alone, and you can stay with me and Mike as long as you want."

"Are you speaking for yourself and Uncle Mike? I'm not sure he feels the same way you do."

Pearl reached across the table and took Marie's hand, "There's not a better man on the face of this planet than your Uncle Mike. He may not always show his feelings, but I know he cares for you the same as I do."

"Okay, Aunt Pearl," Marie said smiling. "But I have something you can help me with."

"What is it honey."

"I want to visit my best friend in Dewey."

Pearl shrugged her shoulders, "Where's that?"

"About fifteen minutes from Rehoboth Beach."

"It's a good time to be at the beach." Pearl smiled and patted Marie's hand, "And it would be good for you to visit your friend."

"Yeah, I tried to find a bus that goes there, but I'd have to leave from DC, and it won't work on the train either."

"How are you going to get there?"

"I have a credit card, and could rent a car."

Pearl leaned close to Marie, "Do you need me to give you money?"

"No, you've done enough for me, but could you help me find a car rental?"

Pearl laughed, "Child, you asking the wrong one—I've never rented a car. But let's get the yellow pages and call places."

The two women called several companies until they found one located downtown that had a car Marie could afford. Pearl drove her niece to the car rental office and stood by as Marie received instructions on the automobile and signed the contract.

"Are you sure you going to be okay driving by yourself in this little car?

"Marie laughed, "I drove Aunt Tissy's beat-up old car from Philly to Dewey. This car is a dream in comparison," she chuckled. "Don't worry, I'll be okay."

"Make sure you call when you get there to let us know you are okay."

"Okay, Aunt Pearl," Marie answered smiling.

***

Pearl took her time driving home. Most of the time Mike drove, but she did not want to interrupt him. She also hesitated to ask since it was for Marie. Mike did not trust his niece, and Pearl wondered if she was making a mistake since everyone else was skeptical of Marie. There was sadness surrounding the young woman that touched Pearl's heart. Brenda as a mother was bad enough, but it sounded as if the father wasn't a jewel either, Pearl reasoned.

"Maybe I'm wrong?" She asked herself, but decided she would continue to show her niece kindness despite the criticism.

CHAPTER 19

Walter walked into the front door and observed Asia's stepdaughter reading a book to a group of young kids. He watched the little freckled-face red-haired child and chuckled at her level of animation as she read the story with the kids repeating her words and actions. It was a story Linda read to Asia, and he remembered how much enjoyment his child expressed every time her mother read the story.

He felt a surge of guilt and shame and started to leave. *I can't keep running away.* Walter continued walking through the center and noticed a small room on his left. Several kids were sitting at a table eating cereal, fruit, and drinking juice. Wondering why the kids were eating breakfast when they had just left home, he stood observing the children. Watching them enjoy their meals, he realized breakfast was a necessity at this center.

Hearing laughter, he walked to the back of the building; and saw a basketball hoop mounted on a pole in the rear yard. Several boys and girls lined up practicing their shots as Asia's stepson and Mike assisted them. Walter jumped out of view so Mike could not see him.

Walter headed to the staircase leading to the second floor and his daughter's office, when a little boy about three ran into him. "Whoa, slow down little fellow," Walter instructed.

A woman came after the child calling, "Come here Eric Raizel. Walter, what are you doing here?" the woman asked as she almost ran into him.

"I'm here to see Asia," he stammered surprised to hear the little boy called by his grandson's name. At first, Walter did not recognize the very attractive woman pursuing the child, but upon closer review, he realized it was his daughter's friend, Patty. He had only seen her a few times, and each time she was polished and professional, dressed in business attire. Today she had on jeans, a tee shirt, and no makeup.

"Is the little boy yours?" He asked without answering her question.

"Yes."

"You named him after Eric? I'm sure Asia appreciated it."

"I named my son after Eric and my deceased grandmother," she responded as she held on to her twisting son's hand.

"Why are you here?" she repeated.

"I want to volunteer."

Patty called Lizzie to get Eric Raizel and turned to face Walter. "Haven't you caused Asia enough pain, and why should she let you?"

"She might not, but I'm going to ask. Maybe she's ready to forgive me."

"Good luck, but I wouldn't hold my breath," Patty said leaving and returning to her son.

Walter climbed the stairs to Asia's office and knocked on her half-opened door.

"Come in," she announced.

Asia sat at a long table with papers spread over it, stapling them together. Walter saw the shock on her face as she looked up from the table.

"Walter... why are you here?"

"Can I help you staple the papers?"

"I'm almost finished. They're promotional packages to potential sponsors."

"May I help you with something?" Asia asked.

Walter sat at the table across from his daughter. "I want to talk to you about... uh... volunteering here."

Asia sat back into her chair, "Why Walter, and why now? Since my mother died, I've only seen you a few times." Asia leaned closer to her father, "Are you going to come here, have my kids counting on you, and then disappear? These children don't need more disappointments in their lives."

"Are you talking about the kids or yourself?"

"Both."

"I understand your feelings about me. I've been a terrible father and human being." Walter extended his hand toward Asia, "I wasted my life and disappointed you."

"Walter, when I needed you the most, you abandoned me. Now you have the nerve to come to my center," she pointed her finger, "a place you did nothing to help bring about, and ask me to let you near my kids."

"It's difficult for you to understand. I'm not asking for sympathy, but it was hard to deal with your mother's illness for so many years." Walter walked over to the window and observed a group of boys racing through the street on motorbikes. "I felt so much guilt when you were born and your mother's health declined. Some days she seemed fine, and other days she'd be so sick, I thought they'd be her last...."

"You weren't the only one that had to deal with her illness. That's the nature of lupus." Asia sat back in her chair and asked. "So you helped yourself feel better by sleeping with my mother's twin?"

Walter paused, searching for words. "Brenda was away, and I hadn't seen her for years. When she came back home, she was like a breath of fresh air—happy, carefree and fun." He exhaled, "She caught me at a low point in my life." Walter returned from the window and sat across from Asia.

"Don't put this on Aunt Brenda. She didn't twist your arm."

"You're right, she didn't, but after I began seeing her, I felt so guilty. I convinced myself that you were better off with Mike and Pearl."

"It's true, I was."

"Please let me make it up to you by doing something to help the center."

"What could you do here?"

"I can draw and wanted to go to art school when I was young, but my mother couldn't afford it.

I brought some drawings. Would you like to see them?" Walter asked as he pulled out several from the thin briefcase he was carrying.

Asia looked at his drawings, stopped at one of her when she was about five, sitting on her mother's lap. She ran her finger around their outlines as tears emerged from her eyes.

Her reaction to the drawing reminded Walter of how much he had hurt his child. He wanted to embrace her, but was afraid. Instead, Walter sat in his seat and hung his head.

Mike entered the room and saw Asia crying. "What the hell have you done to her?" he asked Walter.

"It's all right, Uncle Mike. I got emotional seeing this drawing of me and my mother." She handed it to her uncle.

"Why you bring this here?"

"He wants to volunteer to teach the kids art," Asia answered before Walter could say anything.

"Hell no, we don't want or need you. It's too late to be playing father, isn't it?"

"Mike, I'm grateful to you and Pearl for raising Asia and my grandson, and you're right she don't need me." Walter left his chair and took a few steps toward Mike. "Eric was my grandson, and I wasn't a good grandfather to him either; but I'm asking for an opportunity to do something in his memory."

"It's too late if you ask me," Mike grumbled.

"Isn't Eric's Place about helping others?" Walter asked.

Mike turned to Asia. "Sweetheart it's your decision, but I don't think it's a good idea. All he's ever done was cause you and your mother grief."

"You've never liked me, and I understand, but it wasn't bad between me and Linda." Walter shook his head. "The biggest mistake I ever made in my life was hooking up with Brenda, but it was my weakness not my lack of love for Asia's mother."

Mike frowned, "I guess you also stayed with Brenda out of weakness—huh? If you're so weak, why're you here now?"

Walter turned away from Mike and walked over to the wall opposite his daughter's desk. There were several black and white photographs of old entertainers Asia removed from the barbershop and remounted on her office wall. He touched them as he spoke: "Brenda was always the strong one in our relationship. She left last Saturday and I've had time to think about my awful decisions."

"So, if my sister hadn't left your sorry ass at last, you would've never manned-up and came around here?"

"Mike you can insult me all you want. I deserve it, but I want to help. I'll buy the supplies with my money. If I mess up, you can say I told you so, and it won't cost the center a dime."

Asia stood and walked over to her uncle placing her arms around his waist, "Maybe it's time for us to heal and forgive." She directed her attention to Walter, "I'm giving you a chance. Can you start next Saturday?"

"Yes, thank you," Walter said smiling.

***

After her uncle and father left the office, Asia again picked up the drawing. She ran her fingers around the two outlines and recalled the day her mother died.

She was twelve-years-old, and the night before had been rough. Her mother, Linda, was in the hospital, and Asia sought comfort by getting into her mother's bed and hugging the pillow. The young girl went into her mother's closet, turned on the overhead light, and closed the door. Asia crouched on the floor and stroked Linda's favorite fur coat until she heard voices. She realized it was her father, and her mother's twin sister talking in the bedroom. Asia turned off the dim overhead light, peeped through a small crack in the closet door, and listened to them.

"Where've you been? Mike called from the hospital a couple of hours ago," Brenda said as she wrapped her arms around Asia's father.

"Linda's dead, now we don't have to hide

anymore since she's gone. Walter, you love me, don't you?"

"Yes, I love you, but good grief your sister is dead. Was Asia at the hospital when her mother passed?"

"No, my brother sent her home; she'd been there the whole night."

"We'll still need to be cool for a while," Asia remembered her father saying as he removed himself from her aunt's embrace.

"My daughter doesn't even know her mother's gone, and I need to spend some time with her."

Brenda threw up her hands and shouted, "When did you ever give a damn for your daughter, or anybody but yourself?"

"Good question," Mike roared, bursting into the bedroom. "I knew something wasn't right with you two. Both of you get the hell out of my house!"

Walter stood still and crossed his arms. "If I leave, I'm taking my daughter with me."

"Take her where?" Mike blasted. "Walter, you ain't got nothing, and nowhere to take her. Trust and believe you're not taking my niece out of her home."

"That's the grief talking, don't make me hurt you," Walter said as he pushed Mike against the wall, knocking over a clock sitting on top of the dresser.

Mike pounced back, hit Walter in the face, and knocked him to the floor.

"Don't hurt him," Brenda screamed as she jumped in front of her brother to stop him from kicking Walter in the face.

Mike glared at her. "Brenda, you disgust me, Linda was your sister." He pointed his finger, and yelled; "Both of you get out of here and don't come back."

Remembering, Asia sat back in the chair as her tears fell.

CHAPTER 20

Walter left Eric's Place with a big smile on his face. The elated man walked in the direction of the park singing several favorite songs he had not sung in a long time. He remembered how the women once loved his smooth tenor voice and was pleased he could hit the high notes. Still singing, he cut through the park and skipped up the stairs to his home. Nicky met him at the front door.

"Wow, haven't heard you sing in years. You still sound good."

"Thanks sis. Where's your husband? I've good news."

"Sitting in the back, staring at the rose bushes you guys planted." Nicky chuckled,

"Guess he's pleased with himself for planting them without me asking ten times."

"Let's go outside to the backyard. I want to tell you both my news together."

Walter walked out, observed Curtis staring at the rose bushes, and put his hand on his brother's shoulder. "You all right, man?"

"Yeah," Curtis jumped and looked Walter.

"Didn't you hear me come outside and approach you?"

"No, I must've dozed. I'm not sleeping well."

"You didn't look like you were asleep."

"He's been having nightmares, and may need his medicine adjusted," Nicky offered. "My sweetie has an appointment for next week." Nicky pointed her finger at her husband, "And you're keeping it."

"I have good news," Walter said guessing the medicine was not Curtis' problem.

"Okay spill it," Nicky pulled up a chair and sat beside her husband.

Walter announced, "I went to Eric's Place today and talked to Asia. Starting next Saturday, I'll be teaching art at the center."

"Congratulations man." Curtis stood and patted his brother on the back. "This might be the start of reconciliations between you and Asia."

"I'm glad Walt. I know you're hurt over Brenda leaving, but look what door the Lord has opened." Nicky put her arms around him and smiled.

The Lord didn't open the door, Walter thought as he smiled back and thanked Nicky. "The kids are young so I'll teach them simple basic techniques." He paused and shook his head, "I bet I still have sketch books and other art supplies in the storage unit me and Brenda rented."

"Wonder if she removed items out of there?" Nicky asked.

"Maybe, but she wouldn't have taken my art supplies. I'm going over there and see what I can find before I spend money on stuff I already have."

"Good idea, but come eat first. You left before I fixed breakfast." Nicky turned to her husband, "Come-on sweetheart, you may feel better after you eat."

"Are you okay?" Walter asked as Nicky went in the house to put breakfast on the table.

"I think Brenda's still alive." Curtis whispered and looked around to insure his wife did not overhear him.

"Are you serious? She's been dead and buried for a week," Walter replied in a low voice.

"If she's dead, how does she come to my room every night to torment me?"

"Curtis, if she came to your room, Nicky would see her. It's all in your mind." Walter took his brother hand, "Don't let this drive you crazy."

"Come-on guys," Nicky called from the kitchen.

"We'll talk later, Curtis."

***

After breakfast, Walter drove to the storage facility. He entered the room, turned on the light, hoping he could find his art supplies among the stuff there.

"What a waste of money," he said as he shifted through boxes and crates with household goods, clothing, and electronics. The furniture was in good condition as Brenda spent lots of money on what she purchased. No matter how big, ugly, or gaudy it was. He wondered if Nicky and Curtis would want any of the furniture since it was not their style. Maybe they could use the household items he thought, but decided he should wait before asking.

Walter found his art supplies in a small crate and decided it would be easier to take the whole box rather than rummage through it. As he was ready to leave, he tripped over a small chest he had never seen.

Opening the chest, he found it full of letters. The earlier ones were from someone in prison, and the later letters appeared to be from the same person at the Franklin Institution. Each original envelope was postmarked. They were in stacks, going back at least twenty years.

He re-examined the envelopes and realized the letters were addressed to someone named Mrs. Brenda Zackey with a post box number. Who was Brenda Zackey, he wondered?

Sitting on the floor, Walter removed the most recent letter from its envelope, held it in his hand almost afraid to read it. After a few seconds, he opened, and read the letter. He was shocked at the contents:

Hi Wifey:
   Glad to see you last Wednesday. Girl you are
still fine as silk. Well, it's final. I should be home
in a couple of months, and I got twenty years of
good loving saved for you!
   I'm grateful to you for holding everything
down and making sure our baby-girl was taken
care of all these years. The money you saved
will help us get started. You are better than I
deserve, and I love you more than life itself.

   Your big daddy, Leroy

Walter folded the letter, returned it to the
envelope, and put it in his pocket. He sat in
silence with his head in his hands. "I deserve
every mean trick she played on me," he
screamed as tears ran down his face.

His chest hurt so bad he found it difficult to
breathe. He rolled into a ball thinking so many
things now made sense. Walter now understood
why Brenda insisted on paying the storage bill
while she paid none of the other bills. It also
explained why she stayed with him. *I was a meal
ticket while she waited for the man she loved.*
This made things more difficult he realized as
two more people would be searching for Brenda.

CHAPTER 21

Lila waved from her neighbor's porch, came and leaned into the open window as Marie pulled up to the curb in the rental car. Smiling, she stated their invitation to Mr. Rudy's house for dinner that evening.

"I hope you didn't agree to borrow the money from him." Marie felt anger rising in her body.

"No, we'll discuss it this evening."

"I hope he's not cooking. I'd be afraid to eat what that nasty-old man cooked."

"He's not that bad, but no he's ordering from a restaurant for delivery."

"How can you stand him?"

"I've known Mr. Rudy my whole life. He's lived next door to my grandmother forever." She put her finger to her mouth. "Please lower your voice he might hear you."

"I doubt his hearing is that good."

"He may be the only one between me keeping or losing my grandmother's house." Lila opened the car door, "Now please play nice."

Marie removed her bag from the trunk, walked up the porch steps, and entered her friend's home without speaking to Mr. Rudy sitting next door. She wished she understood why it was so important to hold on to this house. Besides the money owed, it needed repairs that Lila could not afford to make on her waitress salary.

Entering the small bungalow, Marie smelled the lingering musty odor emanating from the leaky ceiling in the back bedroom. Lila left buckets there, emptying them as they became full.

The furnishings in the house were sparse. Lila sold most of her grandmother's possessions to pay taxes and old utility bills. On the first floor, a dated plaid sofa stood alone in the living room, and a table and two chairs completed the kitchen. There were three bedrooms upstairs. The main bedroom had Lila's bed, TV, dresser, and nightstand. The other two were empty except for the buckets in the back bedroom.

Marie smiled as she saw her friend added a picture of the two of them to the collection of framed family photographs hanging on the walls of the living room, empty dining room, and hallway. Looking around the house, Marie realized the photos were the only things keeping the house from appearing abandoned.

Lila bounced into the house, entered the kitchen, and sat at the table across from her friend.

"You okay? Are you upset I'm considering accepting money from Mr. Rudy?"

"Damn right I am. What does he want? Nobody does anything without a reason." Marie moaned, "Plus, the money we put into this house could've gone to a new house, and we wouldn't have these headaches."

Lila strode to the back door; the sunlight shining through the window gave her a halo appearance as she turned to face Marie. "Did I tell you my grandmother was a domestic worker for a family in Philadelphia for forty years?" Lila paused and smiled. "Yet, she saved enough to put a down payment on this house, and paid until she owned it." She returned from the door and sat across from Marie. "The money owed on this house is a second mortgage for her medical bills." She sighed stating, "I didn't realize how sick she was, or her financial situation. I should've, but I didn't ask, and she didn't tell me."

"Yeah, you told me about your grandmother being a domestic worker." Marie took her friend's hand, "Lila, maybe your grandmother didn't want to burden you."

"The signs were there. Who would've paid the bills? Not my great aunt, she barely had enough to make it."

"Even if you knew what could you've done?"

"I don't know. Anyway before my grandmother died, I promised I'd hold on to this house."

"I appreciate wanting to keep dying promises, but sometimes you can't."

"I'm gonna try." Lila leaned back into her chair and placed her hands on her head. "Years ago, this block included mainly homeowners, many who
looked like us." She grimaced, "Now most are people who only live here in the summer months."

"It's understandable you have good memories in this house and you want to keep your promise...."

"All the memories... aren't good," Lila interrupted.

"You're right, they're not," Marie responded, remembering Lila's father shot her mother and himself in the back bedroom.

***

Marie dreaded going to dinner at Mr. Ruby's house, and descended the stairs with a heavy heart and strong determination. Her friend was waiting for her in the living room. Lila's hair was in a bun; and she wore a bright red and yellow flowered sundress on her small framed body.

"You look very nice. Too bad, it's wasted going to dinner at your next-door neighbor's house.

"Thanks, you look nice too, except for the scowl on your face." Lila laughed, "You're not going off to fight a war."

"Maybe just a battle," Marie huffed.

"I'm bringing a bottle of wine that belonged to my grandmother. Hope he likes it."

"Who cares? We're the ones who'll need it."

"Come-on sour puss, let's try to have a good time."

"I don't understand why you deal with that old fart? Just the sight of him turns my stomach."

Lila took Marie's hand and looked in her eyes. "After my father took my mother's life, I watched my grandmother change. She was so sad and never got better."

"I understand. Someone murders your only child," Marie explained.

"True, she hated my father to the point it affected her health. My mother loved and adored my grandmother, and wouldn't have wanted her mother to carry so much hatred." Lila walked over to one of the framed photographs she had of her mother and grandmother.

"Some people don't get over it when terrible things happen," Marie informed.

"The hatred didn't bring my mother back."

Marie joined Lila at the photograph, "Do you hate your father?"

"No... I never did, but was hurt and confused he did something so awful. I tried to hate him because of my grandmother, but I couldn't." She ran her fingers around the frame of the photograph. "I don't know what demons he had, but they must've been serious."

"How do you not hate someone like him?"

Lila smiled, "One day I was so tired of feeling pain, I asked God to help me and He did."

Marie shook her head, "I wish it were so simple."

"It's easy. We make things harder than they have to be." Lila wrapped her arms around Marie, "Everyone's gone, except you and Mr. Rudy. I can't afford to waste any more time on hatred and anger." She kissed Marie on the cheek, "We can get through this evening together."

CHAPTER 22

"It's a junk shop in here with these knickknacks and pictures," Marie whispered to Lila as their host left the room to open the bottle of wine they brought.

Lila placed her fingers to her lips when he returned with the opened bottle and three glasses. Mr. Rudy poured wine in the glasses and flopped in a chair across from the two women groaning as he sat.

"Hear the record playing?" he asked tapping his fingers. "Look at this picture of me and the singer, Frank Sling," he said retrieving a framed photo sitting on a table beside him. "People called him Velvet."

"I know who he is," Marie answered realizing Mr. Rudy may have been handsome in his youth, but those days were gone. His gray thin hair receded to the middle of his head leaving patches in the back of his head, matched by bare spots in his short beard. Most of his front teeth were missing. The few he had left were yellow, and he spat as he talked.

"My aunt said he wasn't that good, but had the Mafia behind him," Marie snickered.

"Lots of people would disagree with her," he replied with a frown. "I understand you're staying in Baltimore with family." The old man took a sip of the wine, "There's a section in downtown Baltimore with several great Italian restaurants. You should check them out."

Marie gave Lila a sideway glance, but before she could answer the doorbell rang.

"Should be the food, I ordered Italian since Lila said you liked it," he said to Marie pushing up from the chair and proceeding to the front door.

"I'll help you Mr. Rudy." Lila volunteered as she rolled her eyes at her friend and went to help her neighbor. They carried the food and sat it on the dining room table.

As they ate, Marie wondered what other information Lila told the next-door neighbor about her. She hated to admit the food was good, and the lasagna was delicious.

"I'm glad you're trying to save Ellie's house," the host said to Lila. He continued talking with food in his mouth, "Your grandmother worked hard to get it."

"I promised her."

"We both worked for Mr. Gruno forty years until he died in 1980. I was his driver and Ellie, the housekeeper." Mr. Rudy shook his head, "Neither of us could work for his son, a crazy-acting, brutal man."

"I didn't realize you knew my grandmother for so long, and you both worked for the same people."

"Yeah, we were good friends, but it was a different time. Friendships between people of different races were discouraged."

"My grandmother didn't talk much of her life before she moved into her house."

"After Mr. Gruno died, we considered ourselves lucky to find two affordable houses next door to each other. At first the sellers thought I was buying both houses, by the time they realized Ellie was purchasing one, they had signed the contract." He laughed shaking his head.

"My grandmother told the story many times about the reaction of the sellers when she bought her house." Lila paused, "But I never thought of all the sacrifices my grandmother made."

"She was a beautiful woman and went through more than you can imagine. When your mother died, Ellie had to stay strong for you... for both of us."

"Why did she have to stay strong for you?" Marie asked. "You're not family."

The old man paused, frowned, and shouted with food flying out of his mouth. "Why are you even here? If you had any money, Lila wouldn't have to get it from me."

"For your information, I've contributed to saving the house, and Lila and I will pay you back together if she borrows the money from you."

"If, how else will she get the money?" He pointed his finger at Marie. "What can you do for her, little girl? Stop trying to act like a big man!"

Marie leaped over the table and grabbed the neighbor by his throat, knocking his chair to the floor. Her friend pulled her arm, screaming, "Marie let him go. You're going to kill him."

Lila bent over Mr. Rudy, put her hand on his soaking wet face, and checked his pulse. "He's not breathing she hollered," as she performed chest compressions and breathed into his mouth.

"Let him die. If you save him, I'll go to jail."

"Call 911," Lila said between breaths.

"No, I won't."

"Call damn it! We're not murderers."

Marie went to the house phone and called for an ambulance. They were there in a few minutes, but by their arrival, the old man was coughing and breathing.

"Should I go back to Baltimore?" Marie asked as the paramedics put an oxygen mask on the old man's face and placed him in the ambulance. "He might file charges against me."

"We don't know what he'll do. If Mr. Rudy files charges, we'll deal with it." Lila mumbled, "Wait here. I'm going to the hospital with him."

***

As soon as the ambulance left, Marie went next door to wait for Lila to call her. She sat at the kitchen table with her head in her hands fearful of what would happen when her only friend and lover returned home. Heavy rain and wind beat against the house. She went upstairs to check the buckets and emptied one, wondering how Lila could do this regularly. Listening to the sound of the rain in the otherwise quiet house, brought back memories of the night her uncle died. It also rained that night, and Marie remembered opening the window to let the warm air blow in her room. She could still recall the fresh smell of the rain-filled air.

It was late, and she hoped her uncle would not come home. She fantasized he would be so drunk he would fall down and get hit by a car, or bang his head on the concrete pavement and die. However, minutes later she heard him stumbling up the stairs. Marie turned her light off hoping he would think she was asleep and go straight to the room he shared with her aunt. His footsteps stopped at her door, and he pushed open her bedroom door.

"Don't pretend you're asleep. It's time you earn your keep," he slurred grabbing her by the leg.

Even in his drunken state, he was stronger than she was. Marie pretended to leave her body and was on a beach with the waves touching her legs and the sun shining on her face. Her uncle fell asleep after a few minutes.

This was not the first time he violated her, but she decided it would be the last. The abuse started with him making remarks about her body, touching her, and then one evening in a drunken state, he attacked her. She wanted to tell her mother but was afraid. He threatened to kill her aunt if she ever told.

Marie went into the bathroom to wash his stink off her. She stood there shaking with her eyes closed. Opening them, she looked in the mirror and saw the reflection of four pairs of the ugly nylon stockings her aunt wore to church on the top rail of the shower rod. Marie turned from the mirror, removed the stockings, and went to her room.

Her uncle was snoring. She tied a stocking to each of his arms and legs and attached the other end of the stockings to the old beat up four-posted bed her aunt had given her. She took her pillows, placed them on top of her uncle's face, and sat on top of the pillows.

Marie felt him squirming and dug her heels into the bed as she held on to the closest bed-post. After what felt like forever, he stopped moving. Marie was too afraid to get up, and sat so long her knees ached. She watched the sun come up and wondered how something so beautiful could occur every day in such an ugly world.

Her aunt entered the bedroom and helped Marie from the bed. Aunt Tissy confirmed her husband was dead and told Marie, "Do exactly what I say."

The two women untied the stockings, took off the dead man's shoes and pants, and washed him. Marie removed the two pillows on her bed and replaced them with two from her aunt's bed.

Aunt Tissy placed his arm in a position where the paramedics could see the medical bracelet as soon as they approached his body. She told Marie to go into her bedroom, called 911, and the family doctor.

"What should I tell the doctor?"

"Tell him to meet Hank at the hospital."

"Why? We know he's dead."

"To sign the death certificate so there won't be an autopsy."

After the small funeral, Aunt Tissy never talked about how Hank died. She seldom mentioned her deceased husband. Marie did not see her aunt cry or grieve. It was as if Hank never existed. Marie never told anyone the truth of how her uncle died until she uttered it in anger to her mother.

The phone rang breaking into Marie's thoughts. It was Lila asking to be picked-up from the hospital. Let's get this over she thought, grabbing the car keys and heading to the hospital.

CHAPTER 23

Lila sat in the emergency room alone waiting to hear news on Mr. Rudy's condition. She did not know of any friends or family he had other than her grandmother. Before Ellie died, he was at their house every day, feeding and caring for her.

Tonight for the first time, Lila wondered if their relationship was more than friendship. Mr. Rudy's comment about her mother and his reaction to Marie when she called him on it seemed excessive.

Lila did not know her grandfather, Ellie's husband. Her grandmother said he died when her mother was a baby: victim of a hit and run. As Lila thought about her grandfather, she realized she had never even seen a picture of him.

She wondered if Mr. Rudy could be her grandfather and if so, did her mother know. *That's crazy; grandma wouldn't have kept it from me.* However, it might explain how her mother was light brown with crinkly hair, and her grandmother had a deep brown-skin complexion with coarse hair.

Lila was fifteen when she and her mother moved back in with her grandmother. The young girl missed her father, but not the constant arguing between her parents.

She pulled her legs up to her chest, wrapped her arms around them, and shuddered as she recalled the worse day of her life. It was a warm sunny day, and she was returning from the beach when she saw an ambulance in front of their house.

Lila recalled hearing a horrible-painful scream coming from her grandmother as she approached. She ran up the front stairs, but Mr. Rudy blocked her entrance and took Lila next door to his house.

He left her in the living room as he made tea. She knew something terrible had happened at her grandmother's house. Her suspicions were confirmed as she stood at the window. Lila saw two black body bags carried out of the house. In her heart, she knew they were her parents. Her neighbor joined her at the window. Mr. Rudy embraced her, and the two wept.

The attending doctor interrupted her thoughts as he approached to report her neighbor was stable, but not in a condition to have visitors. He also suggested she come back tomorrow, but stopped talking when he looked in a folder he held in his hand.

"Are you Lila Thomas?"

"Yes I am. Why do you ask?"

"According to this form, you have Power of Attorney for Mr. Rudolph Rudy."

"What does that mean?"

"You are his representative as it pertains to his medical needs. You two didn't discuss this?" He looked at his watch, "Anyway, when you come tomorrow, I will have a better idea of his medical situation."

She thanked the doctor without answering his question and called Marie to come get her. She was glad Mr. Rudy was alive, but wondered why he listed her as his representative.

***

Lila stood in front of the hospital as Marie stopped. The ride home was quiet as neither of them spoke.

"I guess you're disappointed in me," Marie asked as they entered Lila's house.

"No, just wished it hadn't happen."

"Yeah, me too but that old man pushed me."

"Like you said, he's an old man and sometimes old people say stuff." Lila took Marie's hand, "You got to learn to let things roll."

"That's what you do. He insulted me."

"So you almost kill an old man because he insulted you." Lila threw up her hands, "I don't want to argue about this."

Marie pointed her finger at Lila, "If you think I'm just gonna let someone talk to me like he did, even an old man, you don't know me." Marie shook her head, "You can't see it, but something ain't right with him."

Lila sat down and put her head into her hands, "As far as I'm concerned, you were both wrong, but you have to know how I feel about you."

"I know you discussed not only all your personal business, but mine with him."

"Sorry, I didn't think it was serious to tell him you were staying with family in Baltimore." Lila left her seat and put her arms around her friend. "Please let's not fight over this."

"You're right, we still don't know if he's gonna press charges against me."

"We'll have to wait and see, but I would be surprised if he did." Lila took Marie's hand, "Let's go to bed, we're both tired."

"Yeah, I'm getting up early tomorrow to beat the ocean traffic."

CHAPTER 24

Lila rolled over and saw the sun dancing on a note Marie left on the pillow: *Didn't want to wake you. Sorry about yesterday—please forgive me.*

Placing the note on the nightstand, Lila went into the bathroom to get ready to visit Mr. Rudy at the hospital. She dressed, used her key to enter her neighbor's house, and retrieved his car keys. The car was an old Chevy, but it still ran. Mr. Rudy told her to keep the keys since he seldom drove but Lila didn't want to give the impression she was taking advantage of his kindness.

Lila arrived at the hospital and requested the doctor she spoke to the previous day be paged, but was told he was on rounds and would talk to her as soon as he could. She went to visit Mr. Rudy not knowing what to expect.

Her neighbor sat up in the bed and smiled as Lila entered. There were several machines hooked to him, but he did not have a breathing mask over his face.

"Hi Mr. Rudy, how are you?"

"Fine thanks to you. The nurses told me the CPR you did before the ambulance came may have saved my life."

"Do you have a heart problem?"

"Sweetheart, don't worry about the old ticker." He motioned for Lila to sit, "I had heart surgery a few years ago right after your mother died, but I'm too old for another one."

"Why didn't I know?

"You were staying with your aunt and had enough dealing with your mother's death."

"The doctor said last night I am the Power of Attorney for your medical needs. What does that mean and why'd you pick me?"

"I have no one else. I hope you don't mind?"

"What do I have to do?"

"Look out for me as you did last night. I don't want to be kept alive on a machine."

"Who'd make that decision?"

"Don't fret, according to the doctor you won't have to worry about it for some time."

"Okay," Lila exhaled thinking what a big responsibility this was. "I'm glad you're okay... and sorry about what happened. I've never seen Marie behave the way she did."

Mr. Rudy sat back and closed his eyes. Lila tapped his arm. "Are you okay?"

"I'm fine, just thinking."

"Are you going to press charges against my friend?"

He squeezed Lila's hand, "I'm also responsible for what happened."

"Why'd you talk so mean to Marie?"

"I hate to see you with her."

"But I love her," Lila left the bed and walked to the window. She noticed the courtyard below where several people were sitting and talking.

"Do you love her? Maybe it's because she was there during the worst period of your life?" He patted Lila's hand as she returned and sat at the side of his bed. "I've lived a long time, and I can tell you Marie is damaged."

"What do you mean?"

"Lila, I don't know her story, but trust me she will bring you down into her darkness faster than you can take her up into your light."

She shuddered wondering if there was truth in what he said. "I saw a side of her I had not seen before," Lila admitted placing her head on top of his hand. "It's confusing, but I'm also puzzled about your reaction." Lila lifted her head and faced her neighbor, "It's more than you don't like Marie or want me with her."

Mr. Rudy coughed and Lila picked up the water cup, put a straw in it, and raised it to his lips.

"It's hard for you to understand living now."

"Huh?"

"Life was hard at one time for black people."

"It's no walk in the park now, Mr. Rudy."

"I guess you're right." He chuckled, "But bad as it is now, at one time it was much worse." He looked at the ceiling, "I've only loved one woman my whole life, and most of that time our love had to be hidden."

"Are you talking about my grandmother? Were you ashamed of her?"

"Child, are you crazy?" The heart monitored beeped.

"Calm down Mr. Rudy. I'm... sorry."

A nurse tucked her head into the room. "Are you okay Mr. Rudy?"

"Yes, I tried to get up. Bad idea, I won't do it again."

"Everything looks okay," she replied as she checked the monitor.

"You should shorten your visit, so he can rest," she said to Lila.

"Honest, I'm good. Please let her stay."

"I'm sorry, Mr. Rudy," Lila said again after the nurse left.

"It's hard to understand, but we were looking out for each other."

"What about later, when things improved?"

"I never said anything because I was honoring Ellie's wishes." He paused and patted Lila's hand, "If you're in the dark too long, the sunlight hurts your eyes."

"What does that mean?"

"Can I have some more water?"

Lila picked up the cup and put the straw to his mouth.

"It means after we kept our relationship a secret for so long, Ellie didn't know how to tell you and your mother.

"Are you my grandfather?"

The old man paused again and closed his eyes, "Yes, he said softly."

"Did my mother know?"

"Not for a long while, but she knew before her death."

"So, everyone knew but me." Lila rolled her eyes, "How did she find out?"

"I told your mother a few days before she left your father. I think she knew because she didn't seem surprised."

"Why tell her then?"

"It was after she and your father had a major fight. It got physical, and I was afraid for my child's safety." He stopped talking and a tear ran down his face. "I thought telling her I was her father and loved her might have given your mother strength." He exhaled, "I also wanted my daughter to understand why Ellie sent her to live in South Carolina with relatives."

The old man stopped talking and stared into space. "I always felt bad we had to send her away, but it was for her protection, and that's when she met your father."

"I don't understand," Lila shook her head.

"Ellie was a live-in maid and your mother stayed with her. It was fine until our daughter began developing and the boss' son starting eyeing her." Mr. Rudy rubbed his head, "Ellie and I knew how that would end. The son was a real monster."

"You sent my mother away to protect her. What's wrong with that?"

"Our daughter was upset about leaving and thought she had done something wrong. If we hadn't, your mother would've never met your father," he repeated. "She was vulnerable. Like you were when you met Marie."

"It's not the same. If you hadn't sent her away, she could have been harmed."

"True but to her it seemed like she was being punished and abandoned."

"Is that why you got so upset with Marie?"

"I always blamed myself for not being able to protect my child, but I hope I can help you." He held Lila's hand, "The doctor said I can leave in a few days, and we'll still have time to get to the bank before the deadline on your grandmother's house."

"Thank you so much, but I don't know when I'll be able to pay you back."

"You don't have to pay me back and I also want to give you the money Marie paid toward the house." He paused and looked Lila in the eyes, "If you choose to be with her, don't let it be out of obligation."

***

Lila was glad it was a Sunday afternoon and traffic was light as she drove away from the hospital. She still had to force herself to focus. Her head spun from all the information Mr. Rudy—her grandpa gave her.

Deep down, I should have known he was my grandfather, she thought. He was always there through good and bad times, for every single celebration and heartache. Lila chuckled as she reminisced about the time her grandmother took a class to make jewelry. She wanted to set-up a table at the beach to sell her wares. Neither Lila nor her mother wanted to accompany her grandmother, but Mr. Rudy went with her. He packed a cooler with food and drinks, collected Ellie's jewelry, and off they went.

Her grandmother did very well selling jewelry and continued for several years. Mr. Rudy went with her every time.

The phone rang as Lila entered the house, but she did not answer it. She knew it was Marie as she had called several times on the cell phone. Lila took her family album from the mantle in the living room and retreated to her bedroom. *I need time to think.*

She looked through her album wondering if her grandfather was right. Maybe her friendship with Marie formed out of their mutual pain. They became friends during a difficult time in Lila's life, losing both her mother and father and the tragic way their lives ended. She knew something awful happened between Marie and her uncle before he died although her friend would not tell her the specifics.

Lila decided she would accept her grandfather's offer to save her grandmother's house. She hoped for the best between her and Marie.

CHAPTER 25

Nicky opened her eyes in the dark room and sat up on the bed. She felt for Curtis, but his side was empty. She swung her feet to the floor and adjusted her eyes. From a dim light emanating from a streetlamp in the alley, she saw a figure sitting at the window and realized it was her husband.

"Curtis," she whispered not wanting to startle him. "Why are you sitting at the window?"

He did not answer, and she flipped on the lamp. "Why are you sitting there?" she repeated.

"I'm trying to catch her?"

"Catch who?" She moved toward Curtis, and saw he had a.38 revolver in his lap. "What the hell are you doing with a gun?"

"I'm going to kill her for real this time."

"Curtis who are you talking about? When did you last take your medicine?"

"I'm afraid to take it. She may have done something to it."

"Put that gun down and talk to me," Nicky shouted. "Who is she?"

Curtis placed the gun on the nightstand beside the lamp, "I'm talking about Brenda."

"Who... I don't understand. You said she left. Walter said so too, why you want to shoot her?"

"I'm sorry Nicky," Curtis put his head in his hands and cried. "I didn't mean for it to happen. She came into our room, I pushed her, and she hit her head on the bracket," he said without taking a breath.

"Let me get this right." Nicky put her hands on her hips, "Brenda came into our bedroom, you pushed her away, and she hit her head on the bracket you took off the wall."

"I tried to get her to leave."

"Why would she come into our bedroom, Curtis?" Nicky pointed her finger. "What did she want?"

"I don't know."

Nicky stomped her foot and waved her hands, "All those little hints she threw at you, while you smiled and giggled like a teenager."

"I don't know what you mean?"

"What happened to her? Did she leave like you said?"

"No... she hit her head and died."

"Died! Where's her body?"

"Me and Walter buried her under the rose bushes in the backyard, but she can't be dead because she keeps coming back."

"Good Lord, have you and your idiot brother lost your minds?" She threw both her hands in the air, "I saw Pearl in the market, and she told me Brenda's daughter is looking for her." Nicky hit Curtis, "We're all going to jail," she said slapping her husband several more times.

Walter ran into the room and pulled his sister-in-law off Curtis. "Calm down Nicky."

"Don't tell me to calm down. You brought that evil bitch into my home." She turned to her husband. "For forty years, I've been here for you Curtis. If you had stopped her a long time ago, she wouldn't have come into our bedroom."

"It's my fault for bringing Brenda into your home."

"You damn right it's your fault. You shouldn't been fucking your child's aunt."

"Baby, I'm sorry but this is not how you talk or act. I should've been a better man, but I... love you."

"A little late ain't it Curtis. I'm going to my sister's house. I have to get away from you." Nicky opened the dresser drawer and pulled out several pieces of clothing.

"You can't leave me now Nicky, I need you."

"I'm tired of thinking about you. It's time I thought about me."

"I can't live without you," Curtis picked up the gun, put it to his head, and cocked it.

"Please put down the gun," Walter slowly approached his brother.

"I'm serious Walt. If I lose her, there's nothing to live for."

"Sweetheart please put down the gun," Nicky extended her hand.

The older brother shook his head and Walter charged him knocking the gun from his hand.

The gun fell on the floor, discharged, and a bullet hit Nicky in the foot.

Curtis howled as his wife hit the floor and her blood splattered on the same green, gray, and pink linoleum on which Brenda died. Walter grabbed the bed sheet, ripped it, and wrapped it tightly around Nicky's foot.

Call 911 he shouted to his brother, but Curtis was on the floor unresponsive as Nicky wailed and yelled in pain. Walter felt Curtis' neck for a pulse. It was there but weak.

Walter picked up the phone and shouted at the emergency operator, "I need help for two people—one is a gunshot victim and the other is not conscious. Please hurry!"

"We need to be on the same page," Nicky stuttered while wincing in pain, "Tell the police Curtis heard a prowler, dropped the gun, and it discharged." She pointed to her husband, "Put honey on his gums," she instructed before losing consciousness.

CHAPTER 26

By leaving early and missing the heavy morning traffic, Marie arrived in Baltimore much quicker than she expected. Sitting in front of the park, across from Walter's house, she watched the sunrise. Marie thought of the last time she saw such a beautiful sight and recalled she was sitting on Uncle Hank's head.

Troubled, she leaned back in the rental car thinking how nothing had worked out the way she planned. She could not find Brenda, or the money, and may have lost her friend and lover.

The loud siren of an ambulance passing by interrupted her thoughts. It stopped in front of Walter's house. After several minutes, the

paramedics exited the house with a man on a stretcher and a woman with a bloody rag wrapped around her foot. Walter aided the woman, ran back to the house, closed the front door, and drove behind the ambulance.

Marie moved her car to the side street beside Walter's house and waited for the neighbors to return to their homes. She went down the alley behind Walter's house, entered the yard, and found the back door locked.

Returning to the alley, Marie found a rock, and wrapped it in a bath towel she retrieved from the clothesline. She hit the glass in the small panel of the back door; reached in, unlocked it, and entered.

"This is a nice little house, but definitely not Brenda's style—way too bland," Marie uttered looking around the home. Entering the living room, she picked up the photos of younger versions of Walter's brother and Uncle Mike. She realized the man and woman she saw get in the ambulance were Walter's brother and sister-in-law.

Marie searched each room, but found no evidence Brenda was still there or had ever lived there. She went into the basement and found the same neatness and organization as the rest of the house. Turning to go upstairs, she spotted a small wardrobe, opened it, and inside was a fur coat.

She recognized her mother's coat. Examined it, and noticed the monogrammed initials of *BMZ*, Brenda Mae Zackey. Marie found a business card in a pocket that said *Brenda's Things*, the name of her mother's small business.

Convinced the coat belonged to Brenda; she put it back into the closet, closed it, and left by the back door.

Marie returned to her car and wondered what her next move should be, doubting she could share her information with Aunt Pearl and Uncle Mike. They would want to know how she knew about the coat.

Pulling out her cell phone, she dialed Franklin Institution from a card in her wallet.

"Hello, my name is Marie Zackey, and I'd like to arrange an emergency visit with my father, Leroy Zackey for today."

CHAPTER 27

Leroy Zackey dressed for an unexpected visit with his daughter, wondering why she was coming to see him.

"You've got a visit today?" Brian asked as his roommate dressed. "Sunday is my visit day, but my aunt's not coming. Something happened to one of her friends."

"What was it?"

"Not sure, she called and said someone had gotten shot and she was going to the hospital."

"Wow," Zackey said in amazement. "Even old people aren't safe. Hope her friend is okay."

Brian nodded his head in agreement, "Who's coming to visit you? Is it your wife?"

"Believe it or not, it's my daughter."

"I'm surprised, didn't think the last visit went well."

"It didn't and so am I," Zackey responded, as the guard appeared to escort him to the visiting room.

Marie entered the room after exiting the metal detector and charged in the direction of her father with a serious expression on her face.

"Something happened to Brenda," Marie announced with her arms folded.

"Hello to you, and what makes you think so?"

"Brenda left her fur coat at Walter's house. She'd dump her baby daughter, but wouldn't leave her fur coat."

Zackey sat back in his seat and observed his daughter. As in her earlier visit, she was dressed in all black, except she was wearing pants that stopped at her mid leg instead of a skirt. "How you know Brenda left her coat?"

"Don't matter... I know."

"Say you're right. What do you want me to do?"

Marie unfolded her arms and leaned forward, "Walter will be in the house by himself tonight. I saw his brother and sister-in-law taken out by ambulance."

Zackey stared at his daughter with an uneasy feeling before asking, "Did you have anything to do with them leaving in an ambulance?"

Marie rolled her eyes and poked out her lips, "No. I'm not a thug like you."

"You haven't told this thug what you want."

"Must I tell you everything?" She sighed, "Send someone to the house to demand answers from Brenda's boyfriend."

The big man grabbed his forehead in disbelief, "You want me to send someone to Walter's house to question him about Brenda?"

"Yeah, I know the address, he's not that tough so he'll fold with a little persuasion," she sneered.

"Marie, I'm on my way home, and been locked-up for twenty years. I ain't got anybody on the street to do what you're asking." He placed his hand on top of his daughter's, "I don't know if something happened to Brenda. Hope not, but this not the way to handle it."

Marie screamed as she pulled away, "So now the big bad Leroy Zackey's nothing more than a punk!"

The guard approached after Marie's outburst, but her father put his hand up to stop him. "It's cool," Zackey assured the guard. "Marie, please calm down. I'm concerned about Brenda, but we won't find her this way."

"Leroy, I've only got a few days to get that money Brenda claimed to have. If I can't find her, I've got to locate the money."

"So, this ain't over finding your mother. It's about getting the money." He leaned near Marie, "Why's this money so important? Are you being threatened?"

"Hell no," she sneered. "I can take care of myself. You're right it's not about Brenda. What has she ever done for me?" Marie leaned close to her father, and spoke in a low tone, "I'll either get Brenda's money, or I'll find it from some-where else." She rose from the table.

"Marie... please listen."

She rolled her eyes and kept walking.

CHAPTER 28

Walter helped his sister-in-law get into the wheelchair, being careful not to hit her foot. "Curtis is unconscious." Walter hunched his shoulders, "Nicky, what sense does it make to go to his room?"

"Just because he's unconscious don't mean he can't hear me talking to him." Nicky pointed to the blanket on the bed and told Walter to wrap it around her legs.

"I don't feel good rolling you around. You just had surgery."

"Don't worry about me. Did the police talk to you yet?"

"Yeah and I told it like we discussed. Have they talked to you?"

155

"As soon as I came out of surgery, this pin in my foot meant nothing." Nicky chuckled, "I guess they said it wasn't in my mouth."

"Good grief. I must've been with Curtis when they talked to you." Walter touched his sister-in-law's hand, "Sorry about all this: especially you getting shot."

Nicky nodded, "I'm fortunate. The bullet went straight through my foot. It shattered two bones, but it could've been worse." She wrapped the blanket tighter around her legs. "I don't think we have to worry about the shooting, but the Brenda situation might be a different story."

"I'm not making excuses, but I was trying to help my brother."

Nicky put her finger to her mouth, "Don't say anything to anybody. We'll talk more about it when I get home. Now, take me to see my husband," she instructed gesturing her hand.

Walter pushed the wheel chair with one hand and pulled the IV rack with the other. "Been nice if you two were on the same floor."

"Nothing's easy, but I should be released in a day or two," Nicky offered.

As they entered Curtis' room, Mike and Pearl where sitting at his bedside. Pearl left her seat and ran over to Nicky's wheelchair.

"My God, are you all right? We were coming to see you after we left Curtis." Pearl wrapped her arms around Nicky.

"Yes, I'm okay. How'd you know we were here?"

"Are you kidding?" Mike asked with a chuckle. "Your nosey next-door neighbor called our house almost before the ambulance left," Mike shook his head.

"She was just trying to be helpful," Pearl raised her eyebrow to her husband.

Mike snickered, "I'm sure she was."

"I'm glad to see you guys. Thanks for coming." Nicky extended her arms to Pearl and Mike.

"What's the doctor saying about Curtis' condition?" Mike asked.

Nicky wheeled her chair close to Curtis and stroked his hand, "He's in a diabetic coma, but they're hoping he'll be awake soon."

Mike, Pearl, and Nicky continued to talk to each other as Walter sat in the corner of the hospital room, observing them.

***

Curtis opened his eyes and smiled at his wife asleep in a wheelchair next to his bed with a pin in her foot, and an IV attached to her arm. He attempted to rise, but felt light-headed.

Nicky awakened in the wheelchair, "Are you okay?" She asked as she pushed the button for the nurse.

"I need water but it can wait. How are you?"

"We were so worried about you," Nicky tried to reach his water.

"Wait for the nurse. She should be here soon. Where's Walt?"

"He left with Mike and Pearl."

Curtis sighed, "They were here... I've messed up big time."

Nicky put her finger to her mouth as the nurse entered the room.

"Your husband's awake and I've called to have you taken to your room," the nurse nodded to Nicky. "Come back in the morning." smiled

"Okay, I'm tired," Nicky responded.

***

Walter arrived home and discovered broken glass in the unlocked back door. He searched the house, but found nothing missing or out of order. He called the police hoping this would add credence to the story of Curtis thinking there was a prowler when he shot Nicky.

After the police took a statement and left, Walter sat at the kitchen table. He felt weary and placed his head on his arms. Listening to the water dripping in the sink—he cried.

CHAPTER 29

Marie rang the doorbell several times, but did not get an answer. She used the key Pearl gave her, entered, and discovered her aunt and uncle were not home. This was the first time she came into this house and not smelled something cooking or heard music playing. Aunt Pearl and Uncle Mike enjoyed selections from jazz, reggae, R&B, to gospel.

She was hungry and went into the kitchen to fix a sandwich and pour a glass of juice. Besides being hungry, she was exhausted. "This has not been a good day," Marie told herself as she sat back in the chair and closed her eyes. She roused as her aunt and uncle entered the kitchen.

"I'm glad you ate," Pearl said placing her arms around Marie. "We weren't sure what time you'd get home. Are you okay? You look tired."

"I'm good Marie answered in a groggy voice, just worried about my mother. It's been over a week with no word on Brenda." Marie forced a tear from her eyes.

"Oh honey," Pearl tightened her arms around her niece's shoulder.

"You're right Marie, I'm also concerned," Mike responded as he sat across from her. "We need to call Ray back," he said to Pearl.

Marie dabbed her eyes with her finger, "Who's Ray, Uncle Mike?" Marie looked from her aunt to her uncle for an answer.

"He's a good friend of mine," Mike answered.

"Do you think he can find my mother? I'm afraid something happened to her."

Pearl exchanged glances with her husband, "Honey, don't think about it. Go upstairs and rest." She kissed her niece on the cheek, "Your uncle will take care of everything."

Mike picked up the phone from the kitchen wall after Marie left the room, and called Ray. "I hate to bother you on Sunday, but it's been a week and no one has heard from or seen my sister.

"You could never bother me."

"Thanks man. Brenda has disappeared in the past, but not since she's been living with Nicky and Curtis." Mike hesitated, "Even though me and my sister didn't communicate, I knew where Brenda was, and she was safe."

"Don't beat yourself up; anybody would've been upset with her having an affair with Walter while your other sister was dying."

"Yeah, wish we hadn't kept the beef going for so long." Mike sighed, "This thing with Brenda having a grown daughter none of us knew about is crazy."

"Your sister appears unpredictable. How can you be sure she didn't take off somewhere without telling anyone?"

"It's not beyond her, but I don't think she would've left Marie sitting in the train station."

"Could she have forgotten her daughter was coming?"

"I wondered the same thing, but Marie said Brenda purchased the ticket." Mike chuckled, "My sister is extravagant with herself, but she don't waste money on anybody else. Believe me, she'd remembered."

"What about the neighbors swearing they saw her leave?"

Mike grimaced and shook his head. "Brenda left because of an argument between her and Curtis while Walter was at his aunt's home."

"Yeah, that's what the report I read said."

"I've known Curtis for many years; if there was a problem with Brenda, he would've waited until Walter came home to resolve it." Mike sighed, "I know my sister, and she wouldn't have jumped in the car and pulled off without a lot of drama."

Ray paused before answering Mike. "Okay man, I tell you what. I have an associate with his own investigation agency. I'll ask him to see if he can get some answers."

"Thanks Ray, let me know what he charges."

"Don't worry about it, he owes me a favor."

Marie stood at the top of the stairs listening her uncle's conversation, hoping his friend Ray could find Brenda.

CHAPTER 30

Monday's were tough enough Jerome Foster reasoned, without Ray Hollis calling first thing in the morning. The two men worked in the homicide unit before Jerome retired, but had not talked to each other in over six years.

After retiring, Jerome started his business, Results Investigations. The new business was struggling to survive, and he accepted a project his gut told him to reject.

Leaning back in the chair with his hands behind his head, Jerome remembered the call from a man named, Brian Adams, asking did he locate people.

"Yes, I do," Jerome, replied. "Who are you trying to find?"

"You were a police officer in Baltimore City for many years?"

"Twenty-five years," Jerome replied with pride. "What can I do for you?"

"I'm looking for someone who either lives in or frequents Baltimore."

"What details do you have?" The investigator remembered asking with his pad and pen in his hand.

"I have his street name... Mad Dog," the caller informed.

Jerome frowned, dropped his pen, and sat back in his chair. "Is this the same Mad Dog involved in a shooting of a child around two months ago?" The investigator recollected his heart beating as he added, "If so, every cop in Baltimore City is looking for him."

"I don't need you to find him, just someone close: mother, father, sister, or brother. You get the picture?"

"Why do you need someone close to him?"

"It's important, a letter be delivered to Mad Dog or to someone that would give it to him. I'm willing to pay handsomely for the delivery."

"What do you consider handsome?"

"Five-thousand—you'll get two thousand up front, and the rest after it's delivered."

Jerome wished he had told Mr. Adams no, but back then he needed the money. Delivering the letter set off a chain of events that caused Mad Dog, Lamont Tyne's, death; and could have taken the lives of an Assistant State's Attorney, witness, and other innocent people.

Ray learned Mad Dog received Jay's address from his mother through an envelope provided by Jerome. The investigator doubted he would ever escape that error although he did not know it was Jay's address in the sealed envelope.

It was close to eleven when he heard Ray in his reception office. *Let me get this over* with. Jerome moaned and went out to meet his former partner. "Hey man," he greeted. "Come on back into my office."

"Thanks for meeting me on short notice."

"No problem. What's up?" Jerome inquired.

"Mind if I sit?" Ray requested.

"Sure," Jerome pointed to the chair opposite his desk. This reminded him of the ugly scene between the two men when Ray accused him of giving Jay's address to Mad Dog. The discussion became very unpleasant and they were still uncomfortable with each other.

"Several days ago Mike Wallace's niece, who he never met, came to his house looking for her mother, Brenda," Ray reported.

"Uh... huh," Jerome nodded.

"Brenda was supposed to pick up her daughter from the train station, didn't, and no one has heard from or seen Mike's sister."

Jerome sat back in his chair, "Is this unusual for Brenda?"

Ray shrugged his shoulders, "Mike says she's done stuff like this in the past, but not lately; and he doesn't think she would've left her daughter in the train station."

"Were the police called?"

"Yeah, the neighbors saw her leave, but Mike thinks it's strange the way it happened."

"Why?" Jerome asked puzzled.

"Two reasons: it appears Brenda left because of a confrontation with her boyfriend's brother, and Mike doesn't think the brother would've engaged her without the boyfriend being there."

"What's the other reason?"

"Two, she left quietly. The neighbors said she jumped in her car and pulled off without a word," Ray added laughing.

Jerome chuckled and shook his head, "One of those kind, huh?"

"Yeah, Mike says she's quite a drama queen, and wouldn't have left without a scene." Ray moved to the end of his seat and leaned on the edge of the desk. "Here's something else, Leroy Zackey is Brenda's husband and the father of her daughter."

Jerome exhaled and frowned. "It's been a while since I've heard his name—twenty years or more." He paused, "I recall his low-life butt, and always thought he was behind Mag Dog's mother, Tisha, getting beat-up."

"It must've been before my time."

"You were a pup in patrol when he was sent to prison," Jerome laughed.

"What makes you think Leroy Zackey was responsible for Mad Dog's mother?" Ray asked.

"Back then he was running the drug business in west Baltimore. Tisha wouldn't tell me who hurt her, but I figured she was getting her drugs from him. If that low-life didn't hurt her, he authorized it."

"I hear he's scheduled to come home soon," Ray added.

"Maybe that's why Mike's sister is missing. She could be running away?" Jerome asked as he offered his former partner a cup of coffee.

Ray answered refusing the coffee, "I thought so also, but Mike doesn't think she's running. Here's a picture of his sister." He pulled a picture from his folder and handed it to the investigator.

Jerome took the picture and studied it, "This looks like it was taken in the eighties,"

"It was. Mike and his sister have been estranged for a long time."

"I'll check into it. See if there's any word on the street." Jerome cleared his throat, "I... um didn't know what was in the envelope I delivered to Tisha, but what you said six years ago was right. I should've known something was wrong with giving the letter to her."

"It's in the past, man. Don't sweat it. We've all made mistakes."

Jerome sighed, "Trying to find Brenda is going to take me down memory lane."

"You mean because of Tisha's mother, Macy."

"That was a long time ago, how did you know about her?"

Ray laughed, "Come-on man, it may have been before my time, but there're no secrets in this police department. You know they're like a bunch of old ladies."

"You never said anything."

"It wasn't my business."

Jerome smiled and shook his head. "I guess I never really knew you."

"Maybe you didn't, but know I appreciate you looking into locating Mike's sister." Ray stood, extending his hand, "That family's been through a lot."

"You're right," Jerome dropped his head, "They have, and this job's on the house," he added shaking his former partner's hand.

**

Jerome walked Ray to the front, returned to his office, and closed his office door. He leaned back in the chair and shut his eyes. Jerome needed to talk to Tisha, since he now knew Brenda was Leroy Zackey's wife, but hoped he did not have to run into her mother.

He reminisced about how he met Macy. Jerome had seen her in the neighborhood, but never interacted with her. He remembered her curvy soft body and facial features stunning enough to make a super model jealous. Jerome felt God made a mistake making Macy human. She should have been a magnificent bird, sitting high in the mountains under a tree that would protect her from harm.

Jerome was on duty and received a call the night Tisha went to the hospital with a broken nose, ribs, and two black eyes. She refused to say who hurt her, but all signs pointed to Leroy Zackey.

The investigator remembered he returned to Tisha's house several days later to see if she was ready to say who assaulted her. Macy opened the front door, let him in, and guided him into the living room. Her grandson, Lamont, was on her hip crying, Tisha was in another room shouting, and her father was upstairs yelling Macy's name. It reminded Jerome of a scene out of a B-rated horror movie. He took the crying baby from Macy, told her to go check on her daughter and father; he could wait a few minutes to talk to Tisha.

By the time Macy returned to the living room, Jerome had rocked the baby to sleep. She took Lamont from him and said a few words to express her gratitude before bursting into tears. He knew it was his clue to leave, but she looked so distraught, fragile, and beautiful. Jerome took the baby from her and placed him in the playpen sitting in a corner of the room. He gently put his arms around Macy and felt her trembling. They made passionate love on the floor resembling two drowning people trying to reach shore.

Their love affair was hopeless from the start as Jerome was having marital problems with his first wife. In addition, he was not supposed to have a relationship with someone in the same community he patrolled. Somehow, he found the strength to end their affair. It broke Macy's heart, and after all these years, it still troubled him.

CHAPTER 31

Jerome thoughts were of Macy as he drove to a bar called Pee Wee's Watering Hole. He had not been in here for years, but as usual, it was dark inside. The windows remained covered to keep the sunlight out, and the smell was the same: a battle between old urine, vomit, and Pine-Sol, with the urine and vomit winning. Still, the most depressing place he had ever been.

He was relieved to find Tisha sitting at the counter. "Hey Tisha, what's up?"

"Damn, what do you want?" she asked him slapping her hand against the counter.

"Good to see you too. Come sit at a table. I'd like to talk to you."

"Foster, you're like a nightmare I can't wake-up from. What do you want?" she asked again.

"Please, talk to me for a minute," he pleaded.

"The last time I talked to you, my son died," she rolled her eyes.

"Tisha, let's not go down that road. We could point fingers at each other forever." He directed her to a table located away from the counter, so they could speak in private.

Jerome remembered how sick Tisha looked the last time he saw her supporting her habit in the back room behind the black curtains on her knees. Back then, her light-brown complexion was dull and ashy. She had big bags under her eyes, and two of her front teeth were missing. He heard how she had been clean for several years. "Look at you girl, you even got your teeth fixed."

"Okay, you don't have to blow smoke up my ass. What do you want?" she asked for a third time.

Jerome leaned closer to her, "This has to do with Asia and her family. Her aunt is missing?"

Tisha shrugged her shoulders, "What's that got to do with me?"

"I was wondering if you'd heard anything that could help find her." Jerome patted Tisha's hand, "I know if you could, you'd want to help that family."

Tisha raised her eyebrows, "So what's this, a guilt trip? Why'd you come to me?"

"You might know her aunt. Name is Brenda, and she's married to Leroy Zackey."

She grimaced, "He's still alive, hoped his ass was in hell."

"Here's a picture of Brenda. It's kinda old, but it's all her brother had."

Tisha snatched the photograph from Jerome and huffed as she looked at it. "I know her, didn't know she was Asia's aunt, or married to Big Zack."

"The marriage remained a well-kept secret."

Tisha inspected the picture again, "Yeah, I've seen her, selling clothes, jewelry, and other items at the flea market on the Avenue." She returned the photograph to Jerome. "Okay I'll keep my ears open, not because I have anything to feel guilty of, but because Ms. Brenda's cool."

"Thanks." Jerome began to leave, but gave Tisha a puzzled look, "Why do you still come here? Ain't it hard to stay clean being in this place?"

Tisha took a sip of her soda and sat back in her seat. "They tell you in recovery not to frequent the places or associate with the people you used to get high with or around."

"Yeah, that makes sense."

"It does, but being here keeps me grounded. The people in this bar looked out for me when to the world I was a low-life junkie and they still do."

"I know it must be hard."

"Lamont died before I stopped using drugs, and like you once said, if it weren't for me he would've never sold them."

"I'm sorry I shouldn't have said that to you."

"It's true, and I have to live with it."

"Here's my card if you hear anything." Jerome turned walking away, but stopped, "Ah... how's Macy?"

"Good—real good." Tisha smiled.

CHAPTER 32

Jerome heard what sounded like Tisha's voice coming from his reception area. Surprised to hear from her so soon, he left his desk and went into his outer office, but stopped when he saw Tisha's mother standing there.

"Macy... how are you?" Jerome asked. His heart was pounding and sweat formed on his forehead. After all this time, Macy still made his heart flutter.

"I'm fine," she said smiling.

"Me too," Tisha snickered.

"Come into my office ladies. Hold my calls," he said to the receptionist. Jerome escorted Macy and Tisha into his office and directed them to two seats across from his desk. He removed a chair from the corner and placed it between the two women's chairs. He sat, staring and smiling at Macy.

"You're beautiful." Tisha told him her mother was doing well, but this was much more than he expected. "Macy, you've lost about thirty pounds since I saw you at Lamont's funeral." Gushing he added, "I love your hair, it's all white, the short style is becoming." Jerome paused, "Please, can I get you something to drink?"

"Water would be nice."

Jerome scurried to the small refrigerator in his office and brought a bottle of water to Macy.

"I'd like a bottle too." Tisha requested.

"Sure," Jerome had forgotten she was in the room, and returned to the refrigerator for another bottle.

"This your third wife?" Macy asked retrieving the framed photograph Jerome kept on his desk.

"Yes, we've been married sixteen years."

"Are you happy?"

Jerome nodded, "Yes I am."

"Good, you deserve to be happy."

"So do you, Macy. Is there anyone special?"

"No, but I'm happy. I've got a wonderful job, and get to help people."

"Where do you work?" Jerome inquired.

"At The Layette Senior Center across from the park."

Jerome smiled, "I couldn't work with a bunch of cranky old people. Don't you ever want to get married?"

"No, I really don't," Macy answered, shaking her head. "Marriage is more for men than women." She chuckled and asked, "How often do you hear of mail-order grooms?"

"You got me on that, but as long as you're happy." He patted the two women on their hands, "What brings you two incredible women to my office? She's so lovely, Jerome thought watching his former lover blush.

"Tisha has information about Mike's sister," Macy reported.

"I knew yesterday but wanted to talk to my mother first, cause I'm no snitch," Tisha added.

"That's what keeps crime protected in the black community." He turned to face Tisha, "But I'm glad you're here now. What information do you have?"

"Ms. Brenda's car may be at Lil Moe's car place over on Greenmont Ave."

"Why do you think so?" Jerome asked reaching on his desk for his pad and pen.

"This girl Moe mess with said he picked up a car last Monday for scrapping. But after he got it, he realized it was too good to junk."

"Okay," Jerome encouraged while writing the information.

"I don't want to get nobody in trouble, and Moe can't know this came from me."

Macy smiled, "He won't tell anyone, will you Jerome?"

"This information is confidential between us," he nodded.

Tisha sighed, "His girl, who name I don't want to give, is mad because she wants Moe to give her the car; but he say he don't have no title."

Jerome placed his pad on the desk, "Yeah, that could be a problem. So what's he planning to do with the car?"

"She told me this African guy is going to buy it and send it to Nigeria, but she said if the African guy can get a fake title, Moe should too."

"Your friend believes her boyfriend doesn't want to give her the car?"

Tisha nodded, "Yeah, she said he just wants to make money, so he's selling the car to the African guy."

"What makes you think it might be Brenda's car?"

"It's a white Camry, clean, with low mileage about five years old just like Ms. Brenda drives; and why would anyone junk a car like that?"

"You're right Tisha," Jerome agreed. "They could get much more selling it.

"You can't miss it on Moe's lot with a bunch of broken-down cars."

"Thanks, I'll check it out."

"How you gonna make sure he don't know I sent you."

"You don't need to worry," Jerome said with confidence. "I wasn't a cop for twenty-five years without knowing how to handle myself." He patted her hand, and smiled, "I'll ask him to look at my car while I snoop around."

"Be very careful those guys are real shady," Tisha warned.

"Are you worried about me?" Jerome leaned back in his chair and laughed.

***

After Macy and Tisha left, Jerome called Ray. "Mike sister's car may be on Greenmont Avenue at a shop called Lil Moe's Car Repair." He looked at his notes. "I remember the place. It was busted for selling stolen auto parts just before I retired."

"How you want to play this, Jerome?"

"Let me check it out, but I have to move fast. I hear Moe's trying to sell it to a Nigerian. If he does, we'll never find it."

"Want me to go with you?" Ray inquired.

"I got it, and will call you as soon as I have something," Jerome assured his former partner.

CHAPTER 33

Jerome entered the lot of Lil Moe's Car Repair and saw the white Camry nested in between several battered-looking cars like a rose in the middle of a landfill. He continued driving a short distance until he reached the front of the small shop. The door was open and two men sat in lawn chairs in front of it.

"Can I help you?" the bigger of the two men asked.

"Looking for Lil Moe," Jerome answered.

"That's me," the huge man stood and responded.

"Can you look at my car?" The investigator chuckled thinking there was nothing little about this guy. "I might have a problem with my starter. Sometimes it starts right up, but other times it won't." Jerome knew his battery was weak and had plans to purchase one when he left Lil Moe's Car Repair.

"It could be a lot of things," the big man said as he walked up to the car. "Turn it off, pop your hood, and start it again."

Jerome did as requested and slid out of his car. He walked away leaving the two men looking under his hood. Strolling to the white Camry, Jerome looked thru the front window, and spotted the VIN number on the driver's side of the dashboard.

He purchased a cell phone a couple of days ago with the new built-in camera. It was a big financial decision for him, and this was his first opportunity to use the phone. Jerome grinned as he snapped a picture of the dashboard through the window and returned to his car.

"Man, good thing you came in your starter and alternator both bad." Moe explained, "You could be on the highway and your car leave you stuck and stranded."

"Wow, how much will it cost to get fixed?"

Jerome had to stop himself from laughing when the mechanic gave him an outrageous figure.

"But since you a brother, I can give you a big discount. You come tomorrow morning and I'll do the work for you." Lil Moe patted Jerome on the back. "I need half the money up front and the rest when I finish the job."

"What time you open?"

"I'll be here by nine."

"Thanks Man." Jerome got back into his car and asked before driving away, "Are you selling the Camry?"

"I've an offer for it, but if the guy don't bring the money tomorrow, we'll talk."

Jerome left the lot, drove around the corner, and called Ray.

"Hey man just left Lil Moe's," Jerome said to Ray as he answered the phone. "Course the guy weighs about three-hundred pounds," he chuckled.

"What you find out?"

"The car's on the lot, and he hasn't been paid yet."

"Wish I knew if it's Brenda's."

"I took a picture of the VIN number with my phone," Jerome reported with pride.

"You have a camera on your phone. Get out of here," Ray said in one breath. "Man, that's serious. Business must be good."

"Like they say, you got to spend money to make money. A friend purchased it for me in Japan." Jerome beamed, "Hopefully, the phones will be available soon in the USA. Glad I could use it to help. Write the number as I read it to you, but you must move fast. The buyer is supposed to come tomorrow."

"Thanks Jerome it would've taken days to do what you did, dealing with different departments and red tape."

"Glad I could help." Jerome said feeling like he made-up a little for the damage done six-years ago.

Through the VIN number Jerome provided, Ray found the owners of the Camry were Brenda Wallace and Walter Jones. Ray obtained a warrant and headed to the car shop with several uniformed officers.

Lil Moe was alone, sitting in a lawn chair with his eyes closed. He jumped when the police cars approached him and attempted to run, but got stuck in the lawn chair.

"Moses Low, I have a warrant for your arrest and the impoundment of a white Camry," Ray said as he approached the mechanic.

"What I do?"

"You're being charged with possessing stolen goods over three-hundred dollars." Ray read Moe his Miranda rights.

"I bought that car. I didn't steal it," Moe screamed as uniformed officers placed him in the police wagon.

***

Ray met Patty at the police station and informed her about Brenda's car being on the defendant's car lot.

"Do you think he knows where Brenda is?" she asked.

"Not sure," Jerome answered. "Do you want to go in with me to talk to him?"

"Yes."

Patty and Ray entered the interrogation room and identified themselves to the defendant.

"A lieutenant and the States Attorney, I don't know what you guys think I've done, but I didn't steal that car," sweat dripped from Moe's face. "I bought it legit."

"Who'd you buy it from?" Ray asked.

"I bought it to scrap."

Ray glared and leaned over Moe, "You expect me to believe you bought that car to junk?"

"It might sound crazy, but after I picked it up I knew it was too nice to scrap," Moe shrieked.

"I repeat who'd you buy it from?" Ray asked forcefully.

"If I tell you, will you let me go? Maybe I should have a lawyer?"

"You can get a lawyer if you want to, but then we can't talk to you. We'll have to wait for your lawyer to come." Ray pointed to Patty, "The State's Attorney is here now, but the clock is ticking."

Patty sat on the edge of the table and crossed her legs. "Mr. Low I'm not interested in sending you to jail, but you have to tell me who you purchased the car from and the circumstances."

Moe put his head in his hands. "I got this call about a week ago, maybe last Saturday telling me there was this car to be scrapped, and I could get it at a cheap price." He sighed. "I should pick it up at an address on Park Heights from the backyard. I get the car; pay this old lady two-hundred dollars and have her sign a receipt."

Ray pushed a pad in front of the defendant. "Write down the address and do you still have the receipt?"

"Yeah, I put it in my wallet. You took it when you arrested me."

Patty reminded the defendant, "You still haven't given me the name of the person who called you about the car."

"If I give you the name, will you let me go?" Moe pleaded.

"You may have to testify if there's a trial," Patty informed.

Moe screeched, "I don't want to testify. I can't come-off like a snitch."

"Okay Mr. Low, then you can go to jail. Don't you have back-up time on probation?" Patty left the table and sat in the chair opposite him. "You can also do that time."

Moe let out a loud sigh, "His name is Curtis. I don't remember his last name, but he lives in west Baltimore near Lafayette Park."

"How do you know him?" Ray asked as he exchanged glances with Patty.

"We went to school together. Back then he was a pretty good football player before he shattered his knee."

Ray placed a pad and pen in front of Moe, "I need you to write that information on this paper and sign it."

Patty and Ray left the defendant in the room writing and went out into the hall to talk.

"Good grief Ray, does it ever stop?"

"It looks as if something happened to Brenda and Curtis is involved. How do I tell Mike?" Ray asked shaking his head.

Patty frowned saying, "Asia told me Aunt Pearl and Uncle Mike went to the hospital Sunday to see Nicky and Curtis."

"Why are they in the hospital?"

"Curtis shot Nicky in the foot when he heard a prowler and dropped his gun," Patty answered rolling her eyes.

"What? So why's he in the hospital?"

"After he shot his wife, he went into a diabetic coma."

"That's convenient." Ray sighed, "I'll wait until tomorrow to go to the hospital. Maybe he'll be awake by then."

CHAPTER 34

Marie stirred as the sun glared through her bedroom window. She climbed out of bed and observed her aunt's garden in the backyard. Admiring the mixture of bloomed white, red, and yellow roses, she watched a bee flying from one flower to another.

She sighed thinking today was Wednesday. Two more days and the final mortgage was due. Yesterday, Lila called saying her grandfather was home from the hospital, and they were going Friday morning to pay the mortgage.

"If you take his money, you'll be signing your life over to him," Marie told her friend.

"Stop being dramatic, Grandpa only wants the best for me," Lila responded.

Marie realized her friend called Mr. Rudy, Grandpa. She became discouraged and considered throwing up her hands and walking away from Lila and her grandpa, but Lila was all she had. Aunt Pearl been good to her, she thought; but she knew her aunt for less than two weeks. She and Lila had been in each other's lives since they were teenagers. They helped each other survive.

"No, I will not lose her without a fight," she responded to her image in the mirror above the dresser.

Marie realized she could not put her hopes on finding Brenda or the money in two days and needed another plan. She considered forcing her way into Walter's house and pushing him to tell her Brenda's location. The downside to the plan was he might not know.

The young woman paced the floor, wondering what she should do next. Walter may not know where Brenda is she thought, but I have to know for sure. "I'm desperate," she told her reflection. "I have to do what's necessary."

CHAPTER 35

Nicky watched her husband sleep as she shifted in her wheelchair trying to get comfortable.

After forty long years, here is where we are she determined as tears slid from her eyes. She thought about Brenda entering their bedroom while she was not home and became angry again with Curtis. She recalled him with a loaded gun to his head, and asked God for help forgiving her husband.

Curtis stirred, opened his eyes, and smiled at his wife, "Did you get any rest?" He stroked her hand, "Nicky, I can't bear for you or Walter to suffer because of what I did."

"Your brother is also responsible," Nicky sucked her teeth.

"He's not, I'm a grown man, and am to blame for what happened."

Nicky wiped a tear from her face, "Maybe no one will find out."

"We have to be prepared," Curtis held Nicky's hand. "Several people are looking for Brenda, and I know Mike won't stop."

Walter entered the room and greeted Curtis and Nicky. "I'm glad you're awake." Walter leaned over the bed, and embraced his brother, "You scared us."

"I'm good, but we need to be on the same page." Curtis pushed the bottom to raise his bed. "I don't want you or Nicky to take any heat if things don't work out."

"Man, we could be worrying about something that may never happen."

"Hope you right, but we have to be prepared; and we have to stick together." Curtis reached out his hand to his wife, "Please forgive me. I love you more than life."

Nicky smiled and nodded her head as she and Walter repeated their accounts to Curtis of how he shot her. She took the hands of her husband and brother-in-law and asked them to bow their head. Nicky prayed and asked God to forgive and protect them.

Entering the room as they lifted their heads was a tall, dark-complexion, slender-built man, introducing himself as Lieutenant Ray Hollis. "Curtis Jones, may I ask you some questions," Ray announced and produced his identification. "May we speak in private?"

"We know you from when Eric was killed, but my husband just came out of a coma and is not well enough to answer questions." Nicky held

Curtis' hand. "What do you want to talk to him about?"

Ray directed his attention to Curtis, "I spoke to the doctor, and he said you should be well enough to answer a few questions."

"You can speak in front of my brother and wife."

The lieutenant removed his pad from his folder and continued, "It's about a 1997 Camry listed to Brenda Wallace."

"What about her car?" Curtis looked at his wife and brother.

"It's been found at a car repair center and the owner said you called him about it."

"Do you mean my car?" Walter interrupted. "The car belongs to me and Brenda."

Frowning, Ray paused before responding, "Yes, Mr. Jones it's also listed in your name. How did your car wind-up at Lil Moe's?"

"Is it a crime, for the car to be there?" Walter looked at the card Ray gave them when he walked in. "Your card says you are a lieutenant in the Homicide Unit. What does that have to do with my car?"

"According to reports given, Ms. Wallace left your brother's house about a week and a half ago driving the white 1997 Camry found at Lil Moe's, and has not been seen since."

Walter moved between the lieutenant and Curtis' bed. "Brenda is very unpredictable, but to answer your question I found the car parked in the back of my aunt's house on Park Heights and asked my brother to scrap it."

"Why would you junk the car when you could make more selling it?"

"I admit, it wasn't a rational decision, but I was angry at Brenda for leaving the way she did, and wanted to get back at her."

Ray hesitated, "Thank you for answering my questions, Mr. Jones." He walked around Walter and turned to Curtis and Nicky, "Hope you both are feeling better soon."

Curtis moaned after the officer left his room, "That's what I didn't want to happen."

Walter looked out the door to make sure they were alone and closed it. "I know Curtis, but like you said, we're in this together."

"Do you think this is the end?" Nicky wrung her hands.

Walter shook his head, "I doubt it. Why would a homicide lieutenant be checking into a missing person case of less than two weeks?"

"Mike." Curtis and Nicky answered at the same time.

"I saw that officer at Eric's funeral talking to Mike, and again at the opening. I think his wife is a good friend of Asia." Walter sighed, "We have to be careful, very careful."

***

Ray left the hospital and drove to Patty's office in the courthouse in downtown Baltimore. He smiled at his wife as he entered the reception office. She was on the phone, and he made a mental note to talk to her this evening about when she would stop working. His wife could barely fit behind her desk and he hoped she had raised her feet.

Jay pointed for him to go into Patty's office after he bent and kissed her on the forehead. The State's Attorney was also on the phone and pointed to a chair across from her desk.

"What's up?" Patty asked ending her call.

"I just left Curtis, his wife, and Asia's father, Walter at the hospital.

"Did you find out anything useful?"

"Yeah, I found out they're lying big time. Walter had an answer for everything."

"What makes you think they're lying?"

Ray shook his head, "I've been doing this job a long time. I know when people aren't telling the truth. When I asked about the car, Curtis almost stopped breathing."

"What did he say about the car?"

"Nothing, Walter jumped in and said he found the car parked on Park Heights Avenue, and asked his brother to scrap it."

"It's a late model. That wouldn't make sense. He could sell it for much more."

"Walter had an answer for that too. He said he did it to get back at Brenda."

Patty leaned back in her chair. "He was at the center last week and is supposed to work there this Saturday."

"I can't believe Asia would let him back into her life."

Patty sighed, "He's her father."

"How do we tell Mike that Walter may have something to do with Brenda missing?"

"We don't say anything until we know more," Patty suggested. "After all she hasn't been gone long, and could be hiding out somewhere for whatever reason."

CHAPTER 36

The next day, Walter pulled up to the curb of the hospital and opened the car door so he could help Nicky into the back seat. He folded the wheelchair, placed it in the trunk, and Curtis got into the front passenger's seat.

"It's convenient, the two of you being released together," Walter joked. "Nicky, you would've been released sooner if they could have found you."

"That's right," she laughed. "I had to keep an eye on my man."

Curtis turned to the back seat facing his wife. "You need to be careful with that pin in your foot. It makes me nervous."

"I'm careful. I hope they take it out next week when I go for my check-up."

"Have either of you heard from the lieutenant since yesterday?" Walter asked as he pulled away from the hospital.

"No, you shut him down little brother. You saw how fast he left."

"Don't get comfortable. He found the car."

Curtis huffed, "If Lil Moe had done what he was supposed to do, our plan would've worked."

"I bet Moe saw dollars and realized he could do better if he didn't junk the car," Walter added stopping at a red light. "We need to stay sharp."

Arriving home, Walter parked his car in front of their house and went into the trunk to retrieve Nicky's wheelchair. He took the chair into the house and returned to the car to help Curtis with Nicky.

The two brothers got her in without hitting her foot. They sat Nicky in the wheelchair and Walter turned to close the front door. A figure dressed in all black with a baseball cap and sunglasses appeared and pressed a knife to his chest.

"Back into the house and don't try anything cute, or I will stab you," the stranger threatened.

Walter complied as the intruder grabbed the back of Nicky's chair; and put the knife to her throat.

"Who the hell are you and what do you want?" Walter demanded.

Pointing to the kitchen chair she instructed, "Calm down, sit in the chair, and keep your fucking mouth shut." She tightened the knife to Nicky's throat. "Where's your brother?" She asked Walter as the toilet flushed in the powder room.

193

Curtis entered the kitchen and the stranger pulled the knife closer to his wife's neck. "Who are you, and what do you want?" He shouted moving in the direction of his wife.

"Sit there," the intruder pointed. "Keep your mouth shut if you want your wife to live."

"Who are you?" Curtis repeated sitting in the chair. "We don't have any money."

"No we don't," Walter confirmed.

Marie screamed at Walter as she took off her sunglasses with her free hand. "Where's my mother?"

"Who's your mother?"

"Don't play with me. I'm her daughter, Marie." She pointed the knife in his direction and returned it to Nicky's neck. "Where's Brenda?"

"She left over a week ago." Walter explained, "If you don't believe me check the house, and you'll find none of her belongings here."

"I've already checked the house."

Walter frowned, "So, you're the one who broke in. Then you should know none of her things are here."

"You did a good job getting rid of my mother's stuff, but you forgot her fur coat in the basement." Marie sneered, "Brenda would've never left her beloved fur coat. Me yes—her fur coat, no." She again pointed the knife in Walter's direction. "If you don't know where she is, I bet you can tell me where the money is stashed."

"How would I know where your mother has hidden money?" Walter shouted.

"If you don't, you're dumber than I thought."

"So, it's about the money you think your mother has?" Walter asked shaking his head.

"Don't you dare judge me," Marie again shoved the knife in Walter's direction. "You're the one who left your child to shack up with Brenda all these years."

"Miss, my wife wasn't here when your mother left." Curtis said interrupting the conversation between Walter and Marie. "She don't know nothing." He stood and extended his hand. "Please take the knife from her neck," he begged.

"Sit your ass down and don't make me tell you again."

"Okay, be cool. Neither my wife nor Walter were here when your mother left." Curtis sighed, "We had a beef, and Brenda packed her bags. I put them in her trunk, and she left."

Marie shifted her body as she talked to Curtis, still holding the knife on Nicky. She snickered, "You should've come up with a better story. My dear mother wouldn't have left so easy. You would've had to throw her out, and even then she would've caused a major scene in front of your house."

"Several people saw your mother leaving. Were they all wrong?" Walter asked.

"They saw somebody leave, but trust me it wasn't Brenda." She turned to Curtis again, "I'm giving you one more chance to tell me where my mother or the twenty-thousand is before I jam this knife into your wife's neck."

"We don't know," Nicky cried as Marie yanked her head and moved the knife closer to her neck.

"Why are you holding a knife to my wife's neck over money your mother may or may not have?" Curtis shouted.

"Look old man, I don't have time for your stupid questions. One of you better tell me where Brenda is, give me the money, or I'll stick this knife in her neck."

"You're just like your selfish-ass mother," Curtis voice cracked. "I don't know nothing about the money, but I can tell you where your mother is. You want to know. I'll tell you." Tears formed in Curtis' eyes, "She's buried out there in the back yard. Look you can see her grave through the window."

Marie took the knife from Nicky's throat and turned to the window. Curtis grabbed the arms of the wheelchair pulling Nicky to him. Walter charged Marie, knocking her to the floor. While, Curtis rushed over and kicked the knife under the kitchen table and opened the front door. Walter grabbed Marie, and threw her out the house. As she rolled down the steps, he slammed and locked the door.

"Are you guys all right?" Walter asked out of breath, seeing the fear on their faces.

"Yes," Nicky and Curtis answered.

"Call the police," he directed. "Curt, I'm going after her."

"Be careful, she's crazy!"

Walter ran out the house and searched the street, but couldn't find Marie. He went back into the house. "I don't see her." He took a deep breath and called Mike to warn him that Marie may be on her way to his house.

CHAPTER 37

Marie cut her leg on the pavement as she rolled down Walter's front steps. She ran around the corner careful not to leave a trail of blood on the sidewalk.

Crouching in the alley behind Walter's house, she tore the sleeve off her shirt and tied it around her leg. She watched Walter come to the corner and looked up and down the street, but stayed hidden so he would not see her

After Walter returned to his house, Marie ran through the park, past her uncle and aunt's house, and entered the backyard of Eric's Place. The center had closed, but she could see through the rear window and observed Uncle Mike leave the center. Asia and her stepdaughter were still inside the building.

The injured woman tried the back door and discovered it locked. She went into the alley and found an empty wine bottle. Marie grabbed the top of the bottle and hit the base against the curb. She held the bottle behind her and knocked on the front door of the center.

Asia looked through the blinds and opened the door. "What happened to you?" She asked as blood seeped through the shirt tied around Marie's leg.

"I fell. Can I come in and clean up?"

"Sure. Why didn't you go home?"

"I rang the bell, but didn't get an answer."

"That's strange," Asia, said opening the door and stepping aside as Marie entered the center. "Uncle Mike just left. Don't know how you missed him."

"I didn't," Marie slammed the door behind her and pointed the broken bottle at Asia's stomach.

Lizzie screamed and ran to her stepmother, "Don't you hurt my Mommy."

Asia pulled Lizzie close to her, "What do you want?"

Marie shouted to Lizzie, "Go tell Uncle Mike to call over here in ten minutes."

"You can't tell me what to do," Lizzie stomped her foot and shouted back, "I'm not afraid of you."

"Lizzie please do as she asks," Asia pushed her daughter to the door.

"I don't like you and hope you bleed to death," Lizzie snapped as she unlocked the door and ran out of the building.

"You should teach that kid some manners," Marie said directing Asia to lock the door.

"At least she's not a kidnapper."

"Whatever. Where's your kitchen?"

Asia led her cousin to a small room that housed a sink, stove, and refrigerator. Marie continued to hold the broken bottle to Asia's stomach and removed a large knife from the wooden container on the counter holding a set of knives. She substituted the knife for the broken bottle and directed Asia to the stairs. "Don't get cute." Marie threatened, "I hate to jab this knife into you."

"What do you want?" Asia asked again. "Why are you doing this?"

"You'll find out when Uncle Mike calls. For now, go up to your office, sit down, and shut up."

"I knew you were trouble, the first time I saw you."

"Last warning—shut up!"

;

CHAPTER 38

Pearl was on the phone screaming as Mike entered the house, "Oh, my God! Here he is Walter." She shoved the phone to her husband.

Mike frowned as he accepted the phone from his wife, "What's going on Walter?"

"Marie just left here. She held a knife at Nicky's neck."

"I don't understand. Why would she do that?"

"She was looking for Brenda and ranting about some money her mother had stashed." Walter exhaled, "We took the knife from her and push her out of the house."

"Thank goodness."

"But she may be on her way to your house as I understand she has nowhere else to go."

"Good Lord, it never ends. Did you call the police? Hold-on someone is banging on the door and ringing the bell!"

Mike rushed to the door, opened it, and Lizzie ran in the house crying out of breath, "Marie has Mommy. She said you should call in ten minutes." The child ran and wrapped her arms around Pearl.

"We have a problem." Mike returned to the phone, "Marie is holding Asia."

"I'm on my way."

Mike called Winston Augustus and told him to come to his house instead of picking up Asia at the center.

"Why?" Winston asked. "I'm on my way there."

"I'll tell you when you get here."

"Mike you need to tell me something," Winston demanded.

"No one's hurt, but I rather tell you in person."

After Mike ended the call with Asia's husband, he called Ray and explained the situation. Mike asked his friend to call Patty, as he did not possess the strength to repeat the heart- breaking news again.

"Should we call the police?" Pearl asked after Mike ended his calls.

"Ray said to wait until he gets here and can assess the situation, but to call Marie and see what she wants."

"Okay, it should be ten minutes. Call her I'll be on the extension."

Mike dialed the phone at the center, and Marie answered.

"What are you doing, Marie?"

"I came here to meet my mother, but no one has seen her. Walter's brother says she's buried in his backyard," she responded.

"What are you talking about? I'm sure that's not true." Mike huffed, "He was saying stuff to get rid of you."

"Still, I haven't found her and I'm out of time." Her voice cracked, "I need the money Brenda said she had."

"Marie what makes you think your mother has or ever had any money?"

"I believed her, but now the price has gone up. Tell Asia's-loving husband if he cares anything about his wife or unborn child, I need fifty-thousand dollars by ten tomorrow."

"Are you crazy?" Mike yelled. "Asia and her husband aren't rich. They're hard-working people."

"He can afford fifty-thousand. I've seen the car he drives. If not, he can ask their rich friends to chip in: I don't care," she screamed into the phone.

Mike lowered his voice, "Please calm down. Winston Augustus is on his way. I'll call you back in an hour."

"It better not be a minute more," she shouted slamming the phone on the receiver.

"Mike, she sounds desperate and unstable," Pearl, said wringing her hands. "We must be careful not to upset her anymore."

Let's wait for Ray and Patty before we do anything," Mike suggested waiting by the front door as Asia's husband and father approached his house at the same time.

"What's going on Mike?" Winston asked. "Why am I picking Asia up here instead at the center and where's my wife?"

"Marie has her daddy," Lizzie cried running into the living room from the kitchen, rushing into her father's arms.

"What's going on?" he asked hugging and comforting his child.

"Come and go with me honey and let your daddy and Uncle Mike talk." Pearl wrapped her arms around Lizzie and directed her into the kitchen.

Mike inhaled and let out a deep sigh, "Marie entered the center about twenty minutes ago. She is armed with a broken bottle she held to Asia's stomach and sent Lizzie over here to tell me to call her."

"What does she want, Mike?"

"She's demanding fifty-thousand dollars by tomorrow at ten, and she wants you to call her in an hour, about forty-five minutes from now."

"Have you called the police?"

Mike shook his head, "No, I haven't. We should wait for Ray and Patty."

"Wait, that lunatic is holding my wife!"

"I understand how you feel, but do you want the police storming in there doing more harm than good?"

"The girl is unbalanced," Walter added. "She left my house before she came to the center and held a knife to my sister-in-law's neck."

"What did she want?" Winston asked Walter.

"She was ranting about this money Brenda told her she had stashed."

Winston sat on the sofa and grabbed his head, "I knew something was wrong with that girl when she interrupted the celebration looking for her mother."

Mike glanced through the living room window, "Ray, Patty, and Jay are here." He opened the front door and met them. He frowned, "Jay, should you be here?"

"I tried to get my wife to go home," Ray replied.

"I'm pregnant, not disabled. Asia's my friend, and I can help."

"We have thirty minutes to decide how to handle this." Winston grabbed Ray's arm, "I'm willing to pay the money if it keeps my wife safe."

Ray removed a pad and pen from his brief case, "You may need to pay the money, but first we must make sure Asia is okay and stays that way." He directed everyone to the dining room table. "This isn't the usual case where the kidnapper is trying to hide their identity. Marie is a family member." After everyone assembled at the table Ray asked, "Tell me everything you guys know about her."

Walter gave Ray the information about what happened at his house, and Jay told the group how Tommie met with Brian to try to get some information from Marie's father.

"Sorry Ms. Pearl, I know you didn't want anyone to question Brian," Jay said to Pearl.

"I knew about the meeting," Pearl responded. "Brian told me. Wish it had been more helpful."

"It seems Marie is not only upset about not being able to find her mother, but the money Brenda was supposed to have," Ray remarked.

Mike added, "Yeah, she mentioned the money on the phone just now." He turned to Walter, "She also said Curtis told her Brenda's buried in his backyard."

Walter wiped sweat from his forehead, "Curtis was saying anything he could think of to distract her so we could get the knife from her."

"That's what I thought." Mike agreed.

"I can see how she may have thought you and your brother knew something about the location of her mother," Patty concluded. "Sending Brenda's car to be scrapped looks suspicious."

"What the hell?" Mike snapped. "You tried to junk Brenda's car and didn't say anything knowing we're looking for her." Mike stood and pointed his finger at Walter, "It's always something crazy with you and it never ends."

"Calm down Mike. The car is mine. I paid for it, and how would Marie know anything about the car." Walter exhaled before continuing, "I told Lieutenant Hollis, it was an irrational decision." Walter hesitated, "I was trying to get back at Brenda for the way she left." He stood to leave, "Maybe coming here was a mistake. I was only concerned for my daughter."

"Your concern is a little late, ain't it?"

"Mike, we can deal with this after we have Asia back." Pearl wrapped her arms around her husband's waist. "Something bad happened to Marie. She has nightmares and I can see the sadness in her eyes." Pearl looked around the room at her friends and family, "Marie's not a bad person, she's desperate, but I don't know why."

Winston huffed, "It doesn't matter what happened to her, I don't want her hurting my wife and unborn child."

"You're right and I understand your feelings, but like Ray said we have an unusual case and have to handle it delicately," Pearl stated.

"How?" Winston asked in a strained voice.

"Tell Marie you'll give her the money, but you want to make sure your wife's all right. Ask her to let me bring them food." Pearl paused, "Asia has to eat, and Marie might also be hungry."

"That's a good idea; an act of kindness may help more than anything. Pearl, she may be open to you," Ray suggested.

"Marie is closer to Pearl than anybody here." Mike returned his wife's affection by wrapping his arms around her waist and kissing her on the forehead.

CHAPTER 39

"Look at all the cars in front of Uncle Mike's house." Marie sucked her teeth as she looked out the front window of Asia's office. "It didn't take the cavalry long to show up. Asia's in trouble and everybody comes to the rescue."

"What do you have against me? You don't even know me." Asia propped her swollen feet up on the sofa she kept in her office. "We've been nothing but kind to you since you got here."

"We Asia, how have you been kind?"

"You've been at my aunt's and uncle's house for almost two weeks. Have you paid a dime?"

"Your aunt and uncle, last I checked our mothers were sisters. That makes them my aunt and uncle too."

"So, is this because you're jealous of the relationship I have with them?"

"Believe it or not, everything is not about you." Marie shrieked, "Your husband better call in the next few minutes."

"Or what...."

The phone in Asia's office rang before Marie could answer, and she rushed to get it.

"Hello...."

"I'm Winston Augustus. I'd like to speak to my wife."

"You can as soon as you agree to my demands." Marie nodded in Asia's direction.

"What are your demands?"

"Like I told Uncle Mike, I need fifty-thousand dollars in large bills by tomorrow at ten, and not a minute later."

"Let me speak to my wife," Winston demanded.

Speak to your husband Marie directed as she put the phone on speaker.

"Are you okay, sweetheart?"

"I'm all right. Don't worry. I love you and the kids," Asia answered.

"Satisfied," Marie asked, taking the phone off speaker.

"Yes, I'm prepared to meet your request under one condition," Winston instructed.

"You're not in a position to make conditions."

"I need to insure my wife's all right," Winston continued not commenting on Marie's statement. "I'd like Pearl to bring her dinner. She's pregnant and needs to eat."

Marie hesitated as she thought about Winston's request. It had not crossed her mind about Asia needing to eat. She was also hungry, but wanted to make sure they did not try to fool her.

"Aunt Pearl can come, but this better not be a trick, or your wife could get hurt." Marie pointed the knife in Asia's direction. "She has to come alone, and will be searched in case you had anything in mind."

"All I want is for my wife to be safe."

"Call me when Aunt Pearl is on her way."

"She agreed," Winston, reported as he ended the call.

"Are we sure Aunt Pearl should go in there by herself?" Patty asked pacing the floor. "We heard what she tried to do to Walter's sister-in-law."

"I understand your concern Patty, but I have a relationship with Marie and don't believe she'll hurt me," Pearl answered.

"I'm having second thoughts about this. Pearl, you're not trained to do this kind of thing," Mike responded.

"I'll be fine. The main thing to remember is this girl wants love and a little food won't hurt." Pearl smiled at her husband, "I made chicken salad today. I'll take sandwiches, sweet tea, and slices of lemon cake."

"I appreciate this Pearl, but please don't put yourself in any danger. Just try to keep Marie calm if you can." Winston hugged Asia's aunt.

"You don't need to thank me. I love Asia and I will make sure she and your unborn child are safe."

"Winston's right." Ray interrupted, "If it gets out of control in there...."

"I got this Ray, don't worry." She turned to her husband and repeated, "I'll be fine."

Winston moaned and grabbed his forehead, "I forgot to get Win from soccer practice."

"He's okay," Jay assured. "I asked Thelma to get him when she picked up Marcus. I hope you don't mind?"

"Thanks, but how did you know to ask her?"

"I was talking to Thelma when Patty received the call about Asia. I figured you wouldn't mind and forgot to tell you."

"He doesn't know yet does he?"

"No," Jay shook her head.

"Good, I want to tell him myself. Do you think Thelma would mind bringing him here?"

"Of course not, it may also be a good idea for Tommie to come since he talked to Brian about Marie's father. Brian may have told him something, he doesn't realize is important," Jay added.

"When you call Thelma, ask them to park around the corner, and come in the back." Ray said to Jay as he shook his head. "I should've thought of this earlier, but Marie can see the house from the window of the center." He sighed, "Don't want her seeing too many people coming in, it may raise her anxiety level."

"Okay after I talk to Thelma, I'll help you get the food together Ms. Pearl." Jay said leaving the dining room table and following Pearl into the kitchen.

Asia, sat on the couch with her eyes closed and feet up. Marie positioned herself where she was close to the office door but could keep her eyes on her cousin. She used her cell phone to dial Lila.

"Hello," she whispered when Lila answered. "What time are you going to the bank tomorrow?

"Why're you whispering?"

"It's a long story."

"What time's the meeting?"

"One."

"Good, when you get there call and give me the bank's information so I can wire the money to stop the foreclosure.

"You've got the money?"

"Not yet, but I'll have it by tomorrow."

"Okay, I'll call you."

"Who was on the phone?" Lila's grandfather asked as she ended the call.

"It was Marie. She wished us luck."

"See, I told you she would come around," he smiled at his granddaughter. "Did you tell her about our plans to sell my house and use the money to fix-up your grandmother's?"

"Not yet."

"I guess you should tell her soon since we'll all be living together."

CHAPTER 40

Win entered the house through the rear door and stepped into the kitchen with Thelma, Shelia, and Tommie behind him.

Lizzie ran to her big brother exclaiming, "That crazy woman has Mommy."

"What's she talking about?" Win asked his father entering the kitchen.

Winston took a deep breath, "The woman who came here last Saturday is holding your mother and demanding money."

Win's voice cracked and his eyes watered, "Whatever it is, give it to her."

"I will son, but we have to make sure she doesn't take the money and hurt your mother, anyway. We must be strong and stay calm."

"Okay," the young man said as he entered the dining room with his father. "What can I do?"

"It would be helpful if you took your sister upstairs as we try to work this out."

"Why I have to go upstairs?" Lizzie pouted. "I'm not a baby. I'm ten and was the one who told you what was happening."

Win put his arms around his sister, "Lizzie please, let's go upstairs and Dad will call us if anything new develops."

"Dad, please call us if anything occurs," Lizzie begged.

"Thank you for picking up my son, and for coming." Winston nodded his head to Thelma, and spoke to Tommie. "Jay told us about your meeting with Brian, but could you give us your spin on the meeting ...."

"We would appreciate anything you can tell us about who Marie is and what we may be dealing with," Ray interrupted as Patty nodded.

Tommie remembered the last time he had a meeting with Ray Hollis and Patty Lagrue. It was after Eric died, and the circumstances were very different. At that time, the then homicide detective and Assistant State's Attorney were trying to bury him. Now, they were asking for his help. *Funny how time changes things.*

The information he gave then was about the same man Jay asked him to meet, Brian (Glenn Peck) Adams. Tommie recalled how threatening and cold Patty treated him the first time they met until he gave her important information about Brian and Ms. Pearl. He replayed how Patty jumped out of her seat and leaned across the table toward him. Her face was so close he could smell her minty-scented breath.

Tommie focused on the present and gave the group the information he received from Brian, "I don't think Marie's father was involved in Brenda's disappearance, but his daughter rattled him." He reached down and held Thelma's hand, "Brian told me Zackey was not only surprised but disturbed by her visit."

"I think we have learned everything we gonna find out right now." Pearl stood, "I need to leave before too much time passes. Please call the kids downstairs."

Win and Lizzie came down and everyone held hands and formed a big circle while Mike prayed for Asia and Pearl's safety.

After the prayer ended, Walter's cell phone rang, and he excused himself, "It's Curtis, may be about Nicky." He left the dining room and went through the kitchen to the back porch.

"I want to let you know what Nicky and I have decided," Curtis informed his brother. "This has gone on too long and now Brenda's daughter is holding Asia."

"What are you planning to do?"

"I'm going to call and talk to the lieutenant. If I can get a promise they won't come after you and Nicky, I'm ready to tell what happened."

"He's here with the State's Attorney."

"That's what I mean. They're close to Mike; and won't quit until they find out what happened to Brenda.

"Not sure it's a good idea," Walter shook his head.

Curtis exhaled, "I'm tired Walt. Don't forget you were at our aunt's house when she died, and when I buried her."

"Why don't we wait and see how this plays out."

"No, I should've admitted the truth from the beginning. If I had that mad woman wouldn't be holding your daughter."

Walter returned to the dining room as the lieutenant was ending a call.

"Your brother wants to talk. Do you know what it's about?"

"No."

"He said it's important, and I should come to his house now." Ray frowned at Walter, "Didn't you just speak to him. You sure you don't know what's it's about."

"I said no."

Ray turned to Winston, "The money is not due until tomorrow. I think it's safe to leave and talk to Curtis." He faced Walter, "You and your brother live nearby, don't you?"

"I'm going with you Patty volunteered before Walter could answer."

"Would you like to ride with us Walter or did you drive?"

"I walked. I'll ride with you."

CHAPTER 41

Curtis opened the front door as he saw Lieutenant Hollis and the State's Attorney approaching with his brother. He directed them into the living room and pointed to the sofa. "I'll get right to it," Curtis announced. "I know what happened to Brenda Wallace."

"You do?" Lieutenant Hollis asked moving to the edge of his seat.

"Before I go into it, I want some assurances."

"About what?" Lieutenant Hollis asked.

"I want your promise that my brother and wife are not punished for what I'm about to tell you."

"We can't give you a blanket promise before we hear what you have to say," the State's Attorney answered.

Curtis grabbed his head, "I'm... responsible for Brenda's death, but it was an accident. My brother and wife had nothing to do with it," Curtis exclaimed in one breath. "Nicky was away at a retreat, and Walt wasn't home either."

"Why don't you start from the beginning and tell us what happened?" Ray reached into his briefcase and removed a pad and pen.

Curtis sat on the chair next to Nicky's wheelchair and took a deep breath. "Me and Brenda had a big argument the night of her death. She got mad, packed her bags, and left." Curtis continued talking, stood, and paced back and forth. "Walt was at our aunt's house because she's in the beginning stages of dementia and has bad eyesight. We take turns checking on her." He stopped pacing and returned to his wife's side, patting her hand. "Nicky was at her church revival," he repeated.

"Later that night, Brenda came back to the house and entered my bedroom naked. I tried to get her to leave and pushed her," he shouted. "She fell against the wall." Curtis squeezed his wife's hand. "I had a steel bracket on the wall holding my football plaque and she hit her head on it. I gave her CPR, but she was gone."

"What happed after you realized she was dead?" Ray asked.

"I panicked, wrapped her in a piece of tarp, and dug up the rose bushes me and Walt planted earlier in the day. I buried her under them and replanted the bushes."

Patty shook her head shrieking, "Why didn't you call an ambulance if it was an accident. How can you be sure she was dead, maybe she was just unconscious?"

"Like I said, I panicked. I didn't want to go to jail," Curtis whimpered. "Brenda had blood coming out of her head. I checked she was not alive."

"Where's the steel bracket Brenda hit her head on?" Lieutenant Hollis inquired.

"I removed it from the wall after her death and cleaned it with ammonia." Curtis walked to the corner of the room, picked up the bracket wrapped in plastic, and gave it to the lieutenant.

Hollis spun around in his seat to face Walter. "So the story of finding the car on Park Heights at your aunt's house was a lie?"

"No," Curtis answered before Walt could. "After Brenda died, I moved the car and parked it in my aunt's back yard."

"Moe said he was contacted about the car Saturday afternoon. How do you explain that?" The lieutenant placed his pen beside his pad and turned back to Curtis.

"He got the days confused. I called Moe on Monday. He came that afternoon and picked up the car."

Lieutenant Hollis drilled Walter again, asking, "When did you realize Brenda was dead?"

Walter shrugged his shoulders, "I didn't know, but I suspected something was wrong at the hospital." He shook his head and glanced at Curtis. "I didn't think Brenda would leave her car parked in my aunt's backyard. So as I said, I told Curtis to junk it."

"Nicky just found out, and she persuaded me to call you, Lieutenant Hollis," Curtis added.

"I'll call and have Brenda's body removed from the backyard and taken to the morgue." The lieutenant exchanged glances with the State's Attorney. "In addition, I have to call for a wagon. Curtis Jones you're under arrest for the murder of Brenda Wallace Zackey." The lieutenant gave the older brother his Miranda rights as he handcuffed him. "Walter Jones you're being arrested as an accessory after the fact." Ray also gave Walter his rights as he handcuffed him.

Curtis moaned, "My brother had nothing to do with the murder."

"He's not being charged with murder. If they're no outstanding warrants, he may get released tonight."

"What about my husband?" Nicky asked the lieutenant.

"He'll go before the Court Commissioner for a determination of bail."

"Do you think he'll get it?"

Lieutenant Hollis hesitated before answering, "I don't know...."

"That woman's brought us nothing but pain," Nicky cried. "Please take that into concern," she begged as uniformed police officers placed Curtis and Walter in a cruiser.

"I have to go downtown and write this report," Ray said to Patty as the officers left with Walter and Curtis.

"Drop me back at Uncle Mike's," she requested.

"Okay, I'll be back as soon as I can.

Patty sighed, "Ray, we should hold this information about Brenda until after we get Asia back."

"I agree, talk about bad-news overkill. Patty, there're parts of this story I don't believe."

"Me either, but I believe it was an accident. I guess we'll find out after Brenda's taken to the morgue and examined." Patty exhaled, "I hope for Asia's sake Walter didn't participate in the murder." She shook her head, "But I think he knew about Brenda before you went to the hospital to talk to Curtis."

"I'll talk to the aunt and see what she says."

"If she has dementia, it may be a big waste of time."

CHAPTER 42

"Mike, please call and tell them I'm on my way," Pearl requested with a bag of food in one hand and a pitcher of tea in the other.

After receiving the call, Marie directed Asia down the stairs to the front door, and told her cousin to unlock it. She had Pearl place the shopping bag and tea on a nearby table and patted her down with the hand not holding the knife.

"Is this necessary? I told you I didn't have a weapon."

"Sorry Aunt Pearl, but I can't take a chance." Marie handed the shopping bag back to her aunt and picked up the pitcher of tea. "Go back upstairs," she instructed her aunt and cousin.

Pearl placed a cloth on the table where Asia had been assembling promotional packages, and removed paper plates, cups and food from the bag. She fixed Asia's plate, poured tea into a cup and took it to her. "Help yourself," she turned and said to Marie, noticing her leg.

"You hurt your leg, let me attend to it," Pearl requested.

"I'm fine." Marie answered positioning herself so she could see her aunt and cousin as she fixed a plate and poured a cup of tea. She sat at Asia's desk and ate. "I guess you're a big deal around here," she said to Asia, finishing her meal. "I see you have an award from the Mayor." Marie grunted, picked up the plaque, and examined it. "Feels heavy, guess it's made with good materials—not the cheap stuff."

"Why are you doing this?" Pearl left Asia and approached Marie. "If you needed money this bad, why didn't you ask?"

"Yeah right, like you guys would hand me fifty-thousand dollars because I asked."

"Maybe not that much, but if you had a pressing need we would've tried to help." Pearl held out her hands, "Why do you want so much money, what's going on?"

"Fifty-thousand is not much money?"

"It is for us?"

"Her husband can afford it," Marie pointed to Asia.

"How do you know?"

"I know."

"Do you, or is it you don't care?" Pearl returned to the sofa and sat beside Asia. "You still didn't answer my question. Why do you need the money?"

"You wouldn't understand."

"I wouldn't," Pearl repeated. "How can you do something this horrible and not be able to explain?"

"She can't explain Aunt Pearl because being a thug is not explainable," Asia commented.

Marie screamed, and picked up the knife she placed on the desk in front of her, "Shut up Asia! Don't make me come over there and stick this knife in your stomach."

"Calm down Marie. It's going to be a long night. Let's try to get along," Pearl coaxed.

Marie sat back in the chair, "Tell her to keep her mouth shut, Aunt Pearl. It's easy for her to call me a thug, she's always had people to support her."

"I'm tired of hearing you whine about not having anyone to support her." Asia said as she removed her feet from the sofa and placed them on the floor. She pointed her finger at Marie, "If it's true, blame your mother and father, not us. At least you had them."

"You have a father; he's been screwing my mother for nineteen years."

Asia jumped up, and headed in the direction of her cousin. Pearl grabbed her niece and returned her to the sofa.

"That was mean Marie," Pearl said comforting Asia. "How could you, don't you have any feelings?"

"Yes I have feelings." Marie yelled. Asia's not the only person to suffer. I was raped more than once by my uncle when I was only fifteen and my aunt did nothing to stop him!"

"I'm sorry about what happened to you, but it doesn't excuse what you're doing." Pearl left Asia and approached Marie, stopping when the young woman picked up the knife again from the desk.

"I don't need any sympathy, besides he's dead. I made sure of that, and will do the same to Asia if she don't keep her mouth shut, Aunt Pearl." Marie directed the knife in her cousin's direction.

"Did his death make you feel better? Does it help you forget the pain he inflicted on you?"

"Aunt Pearl you sound like my father with his let me help you heal bullshit."

Pearl walked to the edge of Asia's desk, "He could feel guilty about not being there for you."

"He should, so should Brenda, and my Aunt Tissy."

"If you're so angry with your mother why did you come here?" Pearl inquired.

Not responding to her aunt's question and still holding the knife in her hand, Marie moved to the framed black and white photographs Asia had on the wall. She turned on an angle so she could see if either Aunt Pearl or Asia made any sudden moves as she ran her fingers around the frames.

"Those photographs are of past entertainers of the 50's and 60's," Pearl explained. "They were mounted on the wall of the barbershop in which Eric died."

Marie turned to her aunt and asked, "Why keep and hang them?" She looked around her aunt at her cousin, "What a stupid thing to do. Why'd you bring your pain with you?"

"Shows how much you know," Asia replied. "Those photos are a part of our history and a memento to my son." She sighed, "But then you never loved anybody or had anybody love you, so I don't expect you to understand."

"You self-righteous bitch, for your information, I have someone who loves me unconditionally." Marie returned to the desk, "I'm doing this for her to help save her grandmother's house."

"Marie, people lose houses all the time, you don't kidnap your cousin and blackmail your family to save someone else's home."

"You don't understand Aunt Pearl," Marie cried, "If I don't, her grandfather will give her the money."

"Good. He's her grandfather," Pearl clarified.

"He'll use that as an excuse to break us up."

"So much for unconditional love," Asia rolled her eyes.

"I hate you," Marie screamed as she charged toward Asia holding the knife in her hand.

Pearl screamed, retrieved the plaque, raised it, and hit her niece in the back of the head. Marie fell to one knee and Pearl hit her again knocking her to the floor. Marie dropped the knife, and it slid across the tile floor.

"Lord, please don't let me have killed this child," Pearl grabbed a towel from the bathroom and pressed it to Marie's head. "Call an ambulance, your husband, and uncle," she shouted to Asia."

"I'm sorry Aunt Pearl," Marie uttered before she lost consciousness.

CHAPTER 43

The phone rang as Mike opened the front door for Ray. Mike left his friend as he hurried to answer. "What... what are you saying?" Mike repeated. "Something happened at the center! Asia said come now," he announced as he ended the call.

Patty and the kids were asleep on the sofa. Awakening she lifted her head, "Is she okay?"

"I think so, she said come now!" Mike repeated. Ray heard a siren approaching as they hurried to the center and realized someone was hurt. He prayed it wasn't Aunt Pearl as Asia was on the phone. He second-guessed his decision to let Pearl go into the situation alone.

Once inside the center, Winston and his kids ran up the stairs to Asia's office. She was sitting on the couch clutching her arms and rocking back and forth.

"Are you okay?" Winston asked as Lizzie, and Win embraced her.

"She was going to kill me. Aunt Pearl saved my life," Asia stuttered.

Pearl sat on the floor pressing a towel against Marie's head. "I messed up," she said. "I let things get out of hand."

"Asia's safe. Looks like you did a good job." Mike reached and helped his wife off the floor.

"I've got this until the ambulance arrives," Ray said removing the towel from Pearl's shaking hands. "You did great."

"Yes," Patty added as she ran to the front door and directed the paramedics up to the office.

Asia hugged her husband and children as she remembered what happened six years ago when the ambulance came to this location. Her son, Eric had blood on the front of his shirt. "Are you all right?" she asked as she held him in her arms, but he did not answer; he smiled and touched her face. Her sweet child closed his eyes and his body went limp in her arms. The pain she felt looking in his little face with his fresh haircut for signs of life still torments her. She checked his pulse—he was not breathing.

She gave her son CPR. "Call an ambulance," Asia screamed between breaths. "Please call an ambulance!" She recalled how hard she worked Eric, but he did not responded. The police and ambulance arrived as Asia sat on the floor holding and rocking her dead child.

Watching the ambulance carry her cousin out of the room, Asia tried to feel pity for Marie; but all she felt was anger.

After the ambulance left with Marie, Winston approached Ray, "Can I take my wife home? She will give a full statement tomorrow."

"Sure, she looks exhausted. We pretty much know what happened." Ray patted Winston on the back, "Take care of her."

"Can Pearl also give a statement tomorrow?" Mike asked.

"Yes, it's been a long night. Everyone please go home and try to rest."

Patty asked, "What're you going to do, Ray?"

"I'm going to the hospital to make sure a guard's outside Marie's room." He moaned, "As soon as she gains consciousness, she's under arrest. Afterwards I'm going home to see my beautiful wife."

"See you tomorrow, I called John and told him I'm on my way. I looking forward to seeing him," Patty added.

CHAPTER 44

"Higher Pop- Pop, higher," Ericka squealed as Walter pushed the swing he installed in the backyard.

"It's getting hot out there," Nicky stated from the back door. "You two come in and get lunch."

"Not hot, Aunt ickey,"Ericka said not voicing the N on her aunt's name.

"We can come back out after we eat, sweetie," Walter slowed the swing, removed his grandchild, and carried her into the kitchen.

"Will you put her down, she's three-years old," Nicky scolded.

"Me three," Ericka held up three fingers.

Nicky chuckled, "We have a little parrot. Gonna have to spell words if we don't want them to be repeated."

Walter laughed, "If that's the solution, I'll have to carry a dictionary with me. You know I can't spell."

Ericka ran into the living room and removed two framed photographs from the end table. She reentered the kitchen holding them. "You, Pop-Pop," she pointed to Walter. "Me," she pointed to herself in a photograph of the two of them at Christmas time. She continued by pointing to the second photograph, "Aunt icky," the little girl smiled at Nicky, "and Unk Curtis."

"Right, you are so smart." Walter smiled, "Now take the pictures back so we can eat."

Nicky poured Walter a glass of lemonade, "Wait until she sees her Uncle Curtis, she'll wonder who that old man with the bald head is. Did I tell you he has a parole hearing coming up in a few months?"

"Yeah, I think you did."

"I'm grateful to Ms. Lagrue and Lieutenant Hollis for their recommendations. He could've gotten more time."

"He had a lot going in his favor. It was his first offense, and it was an accident."

"If only he hadn't tried to hide it. Do you think Mike will oppose his release?"

"Pop-Pop, look," Ericka brought her coloring book over to show Walter.

"That's fantastic." He looked at Nicky and boasted, "She's only three and colors inside the lines."

"I guess she has a natural talent she got from her grandfather."

Walter placed his granddaughter in his lap, "I think if Mike was going to object, He would've

done it at Curtis' sentencing." He turned to a clean page
so Ericka could continue coloring. "Believe me, if Mike objected, Ms. Lagrue and Lieutenant Hollis wouldn't have made any recommendations."

"The food's ready," Nicky announced as she placed sandwiches on the table.

"Let's wash our hands." Walter took Ericka into the powder room and afterwards placed her in the high chair. "You're outgrowing this, sweetie." He kissed her on the forehead.

"I'm big girl, Pop-Pop."

Nicky placed a peanut butter and jelly sandwich with the crust cut off in front of her niece and her sippy cup with apple juice in it. "This child's high maintenance: cutting the crust off her sandwiches."

"Oh, you love it," Walter joked.

"I expected Mike to be more vocal about his sister's death. I thought he'd be at the sentencing hollering and screaming. He didn't even make a witness impact statement."

Walter chuckled, "Mike knew Brenda and he's always liked Curtis. Now if it was me things may have been different."

"I thought you two were getting along better."

Walter, shrugged his shoulders, "He doesn't frown every time he sees me, so I guess it's better."

Ericka fell asleep at the table, and Walter placed her on the sofa. "I thought she'd go down for the count once she sat still for a minute."

Walter faced his sister-in-law, "How do you feel about Curtis getting parole?"

"If it happens, it will still be several months from now, and I'll be very happy." Nicky took a sip of her sweet tea, "We've both changed since he went away."

"What do you mean?"

"Curtis spent most of his life regretting not being able to play football." Nicky took another sip, "And I spent most of mine pampering him because he lost that opportunity." She sighed, "Since he's been incarcerated, I think he's had to come to terms with who he was and how blessed he is."

"He's not the only one." Walter pointed to his grandchild, "That little girl is my second chance. I've hurt a lot of people, and had to decide who I was and who I want to be."

"You finding Brenda's money and giving the whole amount to Eric's Place says a lot about who you are."

"I would've found the money much sooner, if it weren't so hard for me to face things." Walter snickered, "It took two years for me to throw away the letters Brenda's husband had written. Hidden under the letters in a false bottom of the chest was the money."

"I guess getting old, doesn't mean you stop growing." Nicky smiled, "The best thing for me has been working at the Senior Center across from the park."

"How do you like working there?" Walter threw up his hands, "Not that I'm a teenager, but those old people would get on my nerves."

"You're wild," Nicky laughed. "Some of them can be difficult, but mostly it humbles me. There are so many people who are worse off than us in so many ways."

"Yeah, you got a point."

"Since working there, I've met and made friends with a very interesting woman. At first I didn't know who she was, but after getting to know her, it didn't matter."

"Who is she, does she live around here?"

"Yes... her name is Macy Tyne and she lives in the neighborhood."

"Name sounds familiar. How do I know her?"

Nicky hesitated, "Her grandson shot Eric."

"What!" Walter shouted. Ericka stirred in the next room. Walter lowered his voice. "How can you be friends with this woman?"

"Macy didn't harm anyone. She loved her grandson even though he did a terrible thing, and remember he died a horrible death."

"I guess I'm not in a position to judge."

Nicky grimaced, "There'll be people who will have a hard time accepting Curtis when he comes home." She took a deep breath, "I want to invite her for lunch next week."

"Nicky this is your house... "

"Yeah, but you also live here; and I value your opinion."

"Thank you, you're on a short list. If you like her, she must be a fantastic person."

CHAPTER 45

Marie stared in the mirror as she combed her hair and applied lip-gloss to prepare for her Wednesday visit. She walked to the window in her room and spotted a robin perched on the bars covering the glass. She tapped on the window, and the bird flapped his wings, but did not fly away.

"Are you trying to tell me something?" she asked. The bird chirped and flew away.

"You've come a long way," she said as she returned to the mirror, and smiled. Marie sat on her bed and waited for the guard to escort her to the visiting room.

Aunt Pearl would visit on Sunday after she left her nephew. Marie heard through the grapevine that Brian was close to leaving and wondered if her aunt would continue to visit once he left.

Brian was in another part of the hospital, but he often sent her words of encouragement. She kept his notes and read them when she needed hope.

Lila had not contacted her. Marie wrote her numerous times, but did not receive a response, and her calls were not accepted. The pain from Lila abandoning her ripped the young woman to her soul. It took a long time for Marie to feel anything but hurt and hatred.

A guard arrived to escort her to the dingy off-white cement room with block windows positioned a few feet from the ceiling. The windows were large enough to let in sunlight, but too small for a body to enter or exit.

Marie watched the large-sized man leave the metal detector and walk to her with a slow gait, as he did every Wednesday since she had been at Franklin. For a long time, she sat wishing she was dead, but he would pray and give words of hope.

She was happy and excited to see him, and wondered if what she was feeling was love. Not like the love, she thought she had for Lila, but a sense of gratitude, strength, and belief. No matter what it was, she was happy to feel something other than despair.

"How's my favorite girl?" he would always greet her.

Smiling, she answered, "I'm doing fine Dad— doing just fine."

About the Author

Joyce A Smith was born and raised in Baltimore, Maryland, and graduated from the University of Baltimore with a degree in Business Administration. She was employed by Baltimore City in the Police Department and the State's Attorney's Office for a total of thirteen years. Joyce retired from the United States District Court after twenty-seven years, and resides in Maryland with her husband. To learn more about the author, please visit: **www.facebook.com/Joyce-Smith** and **storytellingpublishers@gmail.com**

Cuts to the Soul and *Cuts Like a Knife* are available on Amazon and Kindle. If you enjoy these books, please rate them. Thank you!